Fath

A

MW01064317

Preface

This book came into being almost like the Greek legend of Athena being born fully grown (and armored!) from Zeus' forehead. Not that it was written quickly or without effort, but that the idea arrived fully formed and without any pre-thought to the making of it. In the first week of writing, I had amassed the first 11 chapters, some 17,000 words. And it was written without any forethought as to the next developing theme. As I wrote, I did keep two viewpoints foremost in my mind:

1) Although it is fiction, it must be Biblically accurate; that is, it cannot contradict the Holy Scriptures.
2) As much as possible, it should fit a plausible Near East Archeological record.

As a casual student of Near East Archaeology (I came very close to postponing my wedding a year so that I could go on a dig in Israel in 1980), I understand the chronological difficulties in making everything "fit" something that a scientific community would accept. I make no claims to perfection, only plausibility. I have placed Abraham in the 21st - 20th Century BC, a young contemporary with Ur-Nammu of the third dynasty of Ur and later with Metuhotep II of the second middle dynasty of Egypt. I use the anachronistic name of Goshen for the Nile river area Abram visited during the famine in Caanan, simply because it is more familiar to Bible students; even though this name probably did not evolve until the time of Joseph, the grandson of Abraham. I opted for the eastern side of the Dead Sea as the site of Sodom and Gomorrah, even though there are those who dispute that. I also took as a real event the account of Abimelech's infatuation with Sarah (which many think is an oral alternate story of the Pharoah episode). In every case, I have tried to be true to the account recorded in Genesis, chronologically and literally.

Let me reiterate, this is a work of fiction, although based upon true events. It was not written with any claims of Divine Inspiration or insight. One of my main purposes was to make the reader understand that Abraham, Sarah, Lot, Hagar, Ishmael, and Isaac (the main characters) were real people dealing with real issues and real problems. I have tried to deal with "stuff" that the Bible does not deal with to make the narrative more alive. I have come up with some possible scenarios that are pure speculation and are probably not the way it happened at all, but could have happened. I purposely skipped certain developing areas of their life, such as the courtship of Sarai, after realizing that if I wrote all that I could think of about them, it could rival Tolstoy's **War and Peace** in length.

In conclusion, it is my prayer that as a result of this book that the One True God be exalted, that the story of God's redemptive power be seen; and, above all, that the reader enjoys reading about a God who loves each and every one of them as much as He loved Abraham, Isaac, and Jacob.

Chapter 1

In Ur of the Chaldees

The stars shone down from the Heavens upon the two shepherds as they watched the flocks sleeping restfully upon the plains of Ur. The moonlit night gave Abram and his nephew Lot cause to be at ease, for no predator could slip among the sheep on such a bright night. They had lost a ewe and her lamb the previous moon, but it had been a dark night with clouds obscuring the sky – a perfect night for wolves to prey.

Abram studied the sky, picking out the grouping of stars the Magi called *The Hunter*, remembering the stories from his mother's lap of ancient times when no stars could be seen in the sky.

"Nothing but clouds…", he murmured to himself, as Lot cocked his head and looked at him questioningly. "Just remembering something mother used to say.", he replied in response to the look.

The two were as close as brothers. Lot's father, Haran, had died suddenly grieving over his wife who had perished giving birth to Lot. Abram's father, Terah, had done the only sensible thing that could be done and taken in the infant, his grandson, and raised him as his own. Lot was some twenty - five years younger than Abram, but the two were fast friends, despite their opposite natures and age difference. While Abram was reflective and serious, Lot was mischievous and reckless. Whereas Abram was hard working and thoughtful, Lot spent his spare time seeing how he could get out of his upcoming duties so he could catch the eye of the several hired girls who worked for Terah's household.

Terah was wealthy. He dabbled in many different trades, which was quite unusual for his day. Most had one trade and kept to it, passing that trade down to their children and their children's children. Terah was more daring. Not only did he keep sheep and goats and cattle, he used those resources to fund trade caravans from Egypt to Ninevah, across the burning sands to bring back spices and goods from beyond the Fertile Crescent. He lived up to his name, "the wanderer", for he could not stay still for long, goaded by a restlessness to achieve more. By virtue of his wealth, Terah had influence in Ur. His two remaining sons, Abram and Nahor, and his grandson, Lot, were being schooled in all phases of his economic empire. Terah brooked no argument, and was known as a hard, but fair, taskmaster; rewarding both successes and failures with an even hand.

Lot sighed. "Think you could see fit to let me catch some sleep for a few hours? I had a rough night last night."

"If father catches you sleeping on the job, you will have another rough night tonight, as well. Only this one won't be rough in the pleasant way your dalliance with that new girl was last night.", Abram quipped, with a mock shake of his head and a wink.

Lot looked shocked, "How did you know...oh, never mind, you find out about everything I do somehow."

Abram responded, "And it's a good thing I do, so I can cover for you when you really foul things up."

Lot laughed. "It's only because you love me so much, brother, and because I am so easy to love... just ask the new girl, Tamirah."

Abram narrowed his eyes at Lot, "I hope you did not take things too far so soon, my young nephew, her father is captain of the guard at the king's palace in Ur. She could be trouble that even I cannot fix, if you have treated her with less respect than she deserves. She is too young for you, and is here only for a season to learn from our mother how to weave the cloth on the new loom your uncle Nahor devised. It is a radically new design that will eventually change the way all Chaldeans make cloth."

Lot dropped his head. "Her father is a palace guard?"

"No, her father is *captain* of the palace guard", came the reply.

"Oh.... She didn't tell me that."

"I doubt if you gave her a chance to tell you anything, if I know you. You were too busy regaling her with tales of daring-do and filling her head with songs of promise so you could get her to let her guard down enough to accommodate your lustful designs on her."

Lot grinned. "You know me well, Abram, but alas; her virtue is intact. But not for lack of me trying to make it otherwise. I suppose it's for the best, though... her father appears to be too... militant, for my taste. I shall have to forgo the pleasure of her company from now on."

Abram whacked Lot on the shin with his staff. "You'll do no such thing! To completely ignore her now is to insult her further. You will continue to talk to the young lady, only now treat her with respect. No more attempts to seduce this maiden. If you cannot control yourself, there is always Bethah... she is always willing and has no virtue to offend."

Lot rolled his eyes as he rubbed his sore shin. "Honestly, how can you suggest such a thing, she is twice my age... and twice my size, too!"

"Only saying, if you can't control your urges... then find a wife, or take a concubine. Stop trying to seduce every maiden father brings into the household. Your ways will bring shame to the family if you happen to succeed."

"I'm too young to marry yet. You know that. We Shemites have a tradition of not marrying until we are at least twenty-nine or thirty years old, and I am barely nineteen. While you, on the other hand, are well past that and still remain unmarried. How do you do it? Are you making frequent visits to Bethah?"

Abram rose quickly from his recline. "This is not about me! So don't try to change the subject. You will control yourself, as I have done until such time as the God of Heaven who looks down on us both and sees fit to bring to us a wife, as He did for Father Adam long ago before the Great Change. Besides, Bethah seeks a husband in the only manner she knows how to, for she is feeble of mind, even if she is not feeble of body. I pity her and would never take advantage of her, as some are want to do."

Lot's cheeks visibly colored, even in the dim moonlight. "I'm sorry, Abram.... I will try to do better. It's only..."

But he never finished the statement, as a distant noise distracted both men.

"Did you hear that?", Lot blurted.

"Shhh! Yes, it came from near the small flock near the western wadi. Let's go! It seems your sleep will have to wait. We must secure the flock, or father will be livid if we lose another ewe or ram, especially on a night like this."

The two made their way with practiced haste silently down the slight rise that served as their watch toward the sound of the noise. It was the middle of the night, a time only thieves and predators roamed the plains. It could be nothing or it could be something. Only a closer look could tell. As they peered over the edge of the wadi into the dry floor below, they spied a young lamb that had fallen onto the washed out gravel below. The lamb was stunned but appeared to not have broken any bones, or else it would be bawling for its mother. The mother had not even noticed her lamb was gone yet, so quickly had the pair of shepherds arrived.

"Selah! I'm glad it's just a wayward lamb," said Lot. "I was in no mood to fight off wolves tonight."

"Nor I," replied Abram, "Let's see if we can get her out without rousing the whole herd. The bleating won't stop for hours, if they start up."

Abram held out his staff as the younger, lighter Lot went hand over hand down into the deep wadi to rescue the fallen lamb. Abram chuckled.

"What's so funny?", asked Lot, as he dropped the final span to the floor of the wadi.

"Oh, I was just remembering a similar scene some years ago... only I was the one climbing down and father was holding the staff.... until he decided that I should learn from this experience how to ascend back up without his help."

"You wouldn't! Abram, it's at least a thousand pace walk to the nearest washout. The whole herd would be up by then... for you know this lamb's mother is going to follow me the whole way bawling for her baby."

"I'm only telling you what happened to me. Relax, now tie the lamb's feet around your neck with your belt and you will have both hands free to grasp the staff."

Abram pulled Lot back up the vertical side of the wadi with ease. "Now, let's have a closer look and make sure the lamb is uninjured." Lot took the lamb from his neck and untied his legs and gently handed him to Abram. The soft bleating of the tiny thing was from fright and not pain. Abram tenderly ran his hands over the lamb's frame. "He's fine, no worse for the wear." Abram lifted the lamb to his face and looked it square into the eye and said, "Let this be a lesson to you. Look before you leap. Not every hole has a soft landing, and not every adventure ends in safety."

Lot chuckled. "Just who are you talking to, the lamb… or me?"

Abram slyly replied, "Oh, did you hear something of interest, too? If the sandal fits, wear it….."

Chapter 2

Terah entered his home on the outskirts of Ur after a morning of business at the King's palace, only to find his wife, Cherah, engaged in a lively discussion with a slim figure whose back was to him. His astute eyes immediately took in several facts; the woman was in mourning for her clothes were covered in ash, and she was not wearing a sash, indicating she was unmarried. He locked eyes with his wife, whose mouth tightened at the sight of him. The mystery woman whirled around and collapsed at his feet, prostrate before him.

"Get up!", he gruffly said, "we do not do that in this home, we bow only to the Lord God of Heaven and Earth."

"My Lord! I have traveled far to find you, so that I may obtain my dowry, that I might not become as one who has no hope or future in this world." The mystery woman spoke quietly and simply, but with great determination in her voice.

"Oh, and pray tell, who are you that I should supply your dowry? Should you not look to your own father for that? Why come here?", Terah retorted.

She rose from the floor of the house, her almond shaped eyes bewitchingly intense, her fluid movement to a standing position made with grace and strength. Standing, she faced him, her alabaster skin flawless, though stained with tears, her stature regal somehow, despite the simple garments she wore, dirty with the ashes of grief. "That is exactly what I am doing, because *you*, Lord Terah, *are* my father.", she announced.

Stunned, Terah could not help but notice her great beauty, and a vague familiarity to her countenance. Well past the age when most women were married, this woman made a claim that Terah feared in his heart was true.

"Where are you from, child?", he softly asked.

"North....the land between the Great Rivers, a small town in the Valley of the Chabur where you passed though on your many travels. You might recall my mother, Shemah, whom you infrequently visited there years ago. I remember seeing you as a child, mother telling me to hide on the roof when you came. Since there was no one else, my mother told me on her deathbed of my father, giving me your name and where to find you. I came, for I have no dowry, no livelihood, and unless I stoop to selling my body to men... I die."

Terah desperately glanced at Cherah, pleadingly asking for forgiveness, or at least understanding, with the look. Cherah whirled and fled the room, unable or unwilling, to remain.

"My sins have come home to rest. Come, child, eat and we will figure this out. Give my wife some time, for she never knew of your mother. She suspected, I'm sure, but your presence confirms her worst fears and makes my life...... difficult, for the moment." Taking her by the arm, he stopped suddenly in the doorway and asked, "What is your name? What shall we call you?"

"My name is Sarai.", she replied.

Abram wearily propped his staff by the door of the large adobe bungalow that served as home to Terah's family. He took off his sandals, poured water from the clay jar next to the door into a basin and rinsed first his hands, then his head, and finally his feet before entering the family room. Seated at the loom was his mother, Cherah, busily weaving a patterned design into the fine cotton cloth she was making. "Beautiful work, mother! As always." Cherah was known far and wide in the land for her intricate patterns of cloth, her thread spun by hand and dyed with rich colors Terah imported from Egypt. The result was a fine linen cloth sought by the rich and influential of Ur and beyond. Cherah was no little part of the economic success of the family. Then he noticed the tear streaked cheeks and the red eyes...

"What's the matter, mother? What has happened?"

Cherah turned to face her first born son. "It seems your father has been keeping secrets from us, my son. It is not my place to tell you of your father's sins, so: Go! Seek him out yourself and find out the truth from him. I will say no more."   She turned back to her loom and resumed her work, her hands flying swiftly with the thread – in and out, over and under – the clacking of the shuttle hiding her sorrow, getting lost in her work.

Abram did not press her for more. He had seen his mother like this before, once after the death of Haran's wife, Abigail, and later, when Haran was found in the plains dead; likely because of the fermented drink he had consumed in his grief. She coped by not coping. He turned to go, but pressed a reassuring hand on her shoulder as he made his way to the back of the house to find his father, who was likely working at his table under the rear window situated to catch the maximum sunlight of the afternoon. "Strange… he's not there.", thought Abram, "but he is always there at this time of the day." Passing on through the house, he finally spied his father in the back field talking to a young woman. He slipped on a pair of his old sandals at the back of the house and made his way to join them.

As he approached, his father saw him and waved him on to them, "Ah, Abram, we have a guest… no, more than a guest; Abram, this is Sarai…… my daughter."

Stunned, Abram took in a quick breath at this sudden announcement. "What? How? Who?", he blurted out in confusion.

"He's not noted for his glib tongue, I can tell you, Sarai. But he is strong, and he is honest, and he is, despite present appearances, quite intelligent.", an amused Terah quipped.

Sarai hid a small smile behind her hand. "I am very pleased to meet you, Abram, our father has been telling me all about you."

"Well, I wish he had told me about you!", Abram exploded. "Father, what is the meaning of this?"

Terah laid his hand on Abram's chest. "My son, this changes nothing and yet it changes everything. Her mother was a woman I met many years ago on my first travels to set up the northern caravan route. She was beautiful, charming, and available; while I was lonely, far from home, and weak. This happened before I dedicated my life to the One True God. I could not tell you what I did not know, for she hid the fact that I had fathered a child. Sarai was the result of that relationship and now her mother has passed to Sheol, and Sarai is alone in this world. She has traveled many weeks down the banks of the Great River to Ur to sue for her dowry that she may marry and live. I intend to do more than that, however, and take her in until such time as the Lord God grants her a husband."

Abram really looked at Sarai for the first time. He studied her chiseled features, her soft auburn hair falling around her shoulders beneath her shawl. He gazed into her green eyes and….. lost his heart. This woman was more than a half-sister, she was the one! All his life he had waited for someone to share his life with, to give him sons and daughters, to love and cherish and to hold; and now, just as He had for Father Adam, God had brought his "Eve" to him. He felt as if his heart would beat out of his chest. But what now? How could he declare his love, here in the back field mere moments after meeting her? Just ten minutes ago, he did not even know she existed! No, better to go slow and wait to see how this plays out.

"Sarai, is it?" "Excuse my lack of manners earlier; as I was, and remain, in shock over the discovery that I have a sister."

"Half-sister", she said slowly. He noticed a lilting accent to her speech that gave her a curious appeal when she talked. He noticed, too, her slim but strong build and her long legs which tapered at her ankles into small sandaled feet. Her robe had been washed and was hanging on the back peg of the house to dry, and she was wearing one his mother's creations from her own wardrobe. Unfortunately it was too short for the taller girl, and gave Abram a rare glimpse of a woman's calves.

"My soul, but she is fine!", thought Abram. "Here is a woman fit for a king!"

"When you are finished with your gawking, son, you can lead Sarai to the servant's quarters where she can rest from her journey. You and Lot will bring her things to the spare shepherd's tent which we will pitch here in the back field for her until we come to a better arrangement… where is Lot, anyway? He should be with you.", said Terah.

"Oh, he went into town to the market to buy food supplies for the coming week out in the fields." "Or at least that is where he said he was going …. I wager he makes his way round to Tobias' Inn for a drink before he returns."

Terah shook his head. "That boy will be the death of me yet. Why can't he settle down and apply himself to the work? Doesn't he realize that his rashness will come back to haunt him one of these days?"

Sarai colored at the remark, knowing full well that she was the ghost of Terah's own past who had come back to haunt him. Abram, noticing the discomfort of Sarai, turned the conversation to the latest prices of wool to distract their father from seeing her shame. She shot him a grateful look, as she pulled her shawl closer to her face.

Chapter 3

"It is settled, we are moving.", Terah said.

Cherah shouted back, "But this is our home! We cannot leave Ur! Our family is here, our friends are here! Our business is here! Why must we leave all that we know and hold dear?"

"We've been over this before, dear wife, and the facts have not changed. Since I publically forsook the moon-god Nanna and started worshipping the One True God, the priests have become increasingly antagonistic towards me, and yes, my family. That's why we must leave! Despite my friendship with King Ur-Nammu, I will not place my family between the hammer of religion and the anvil of state. A war is coming, my wife, and I fear the servants of the many false gods vying for power here in Ur. There are none so dangerous as those who would kill their enemies to advance their faith."

Cherah slumped down in defeat. "But what about our land, our home... my house?"

"It is already done, my love. Sanbat, the fruit merchant, and I sealed the deal for our land and house this morning as we walked between the cut halves of a kid….with witnesses, I might add. It is irrevocable now, we *must* move."

"But Harran? It's so far, I know you favor the place because it reminds you of our poor dead son, but... Harran? It's a month's journey by caravan, even longer for the flocks and cattle."

"Aye, but there's more, sweet wife. Harran has a temperate climate – cool in the summer and mild in the winter. And the grapes! Oh, they grow in abundance. It is on the trade route between Ninevah and Antioch and will make a perfect place to sell your cloth. There is plenty of pasture land for the flocks to graze on, and the area is well watered. Best of all, a large segment of the people there believe in the One True God, as we do. They hold fast to the truths we hold dear, that *you* hold dear. They tell their children of Adam, and Seth, and righteous Enoch.... and Noah, and the great deluge! Why they say that the ark is still visible on the Mountains of Ararat just a week's journey from there! No wonder they hold fast the ancient traditions! God will bless us in this, Cherah, I know it!"

Caught up in his enthusiasm, her resistance faltered. "All right, husband, aptly you are named... you wandering goat! If you had not changed your ways many years ago, I would poison your milk and put on the face of a grieving, but rich, *nu-ma-su* and stay here and wait for the suitors. But, you're a good man now, Terah, and I love you, despite yourself, and will follow you to the ends of the earth."

He clasped her to his bosom and said, "Now, I have only to convince Abram, as well. Since he married Sarai last year, he wants to settle down and begin his family here in Ur. Lot will go with us, as he has yet to take a bride. The change will be good for him. Who knows? Perhaps he will find his beloved in Harran." Terah paused for a moment before he continued. "But Abram holds fast the teachings of the One True God and is convinced he can single handedly change the whole culture of Ur! I fear for him, my sweet, I fear for our eldest son if he stays here. Nahor will remain behind and carry on the business from here in Ur. He has an easy nature and has not made the enemies that Abram and I have with our outspoken views. I know you and Sarai have had your differences, but see if you can convince her of the folly of staying here. Harran is near where she is from, but far enough away that her past will not matter. We need Abram to make this move a success. And he needs to move, whether he believes it or not."

"I'll try, husband. She knows the truth about our God and she is astute, more so than Abram in many ways. And he does love her so… if anyone can change Abram's mind, it will be Sarai."

Abram was worried. Sarai had not returned from the market before time for the noon meal. He had sent his man servant, Abithar, to find her, and he, too, had not returned. Abram made haste through the narrow streets of Ur toward the marketplace, situated in the center of town near the temple of Nanna. The priests had become increasingly troublesome of late to the merchants and patrons of the market, demanding temple tariffs for the "right" to set up shop and to sell or buy in the shadow of their ziggurat. King Ur-Nammu had posted guards to keep the peace, but conflict was coming. Even the blind beggar, Sinbar, had seen that and moved his mat further down the street from the market. As he ran, sounds of more than commerce filtered through the dusty air to him. He quickened his pace. He burst round the last corner to find a mob of angry shop keepers and common folk on one side of the street and the temple guard and the priests on the lowest step of the temple. In the middle was a confusing, milling mass of humanity and animals, where he spied a panicked Sarai trapped by the press of bodies. Abithar was nowhere to be seen. The shouts of angry men filled the air. Evidently, the spark of rebellion had been dropped by some incident and was racing toward the oil of greed and something dangerous was igniting before his very eyes… and his beloved was caught in the path. Abram seized an unlit wooden lamp holder from the street and ripped it from its base, snapping it across his knee to make a crude staff, his favored weapon. Using the short staff, he parted the milling crowd with heavy swings designed to frighten, but not make contact. He could not but help hitting a few people and animals in the process, which only caused the crowd to fall further away from his swinging arc of wood. He arrived quickly at Sarai's side.

"Sarai! Come, let us leave this place! Have you seen Abithar?" With a frightened glace, she motioned toward the temple. Looking up, Abram spied his servant being held in the back by a burly temple guard. Blood trickled from the corner of his mouth, but his eyes were clear as he motioned for Abram to go with a nod of his head. It looked as if they had used force to subdue him.

"Come! Let us get you home to safety! Oh, why did you come today of all days without my sending Abithar *with* you instead of *after* you? I will return for him when this riot has calmed and cooler heads prevail, he will be fine until then. Hold fast to my belt as I clear a path through the street!" Waving his staff in a circle around his head, Abram once again had people falling away to avoid the makeshift weapon. Once clear of the press, he hurried Sarai home.

~~<Θ>~~

"Someone must pay."

The head priest of the temple of Nanna, Dumuzid, took a step closer to Abram and repeated the statement, "Someone must pay for the damages, the lost revenue, and the lost tariffs. Our accountants estimate that two thousand shekels of silver should cover it."

Abram gasped inwardly. "Such a sum! It's robbery, pure and simple robbery!", he thought. He collected his thoughts before he made his argument. "How so? Surely you do not expect me to pay such an amount merely because my servant went to find my wife who was caught up in the riot?"

The priest narrowed his cruel eyes at Abram. "No, I place the cost squarely upon your servant himself. It was he that escalated the riot to the point of no control. And, I might add, your wife was at the center of the beginning of the riot when she refused to pay our steward the required market tariff for shopping. We will excuse her, for she is a mere woman with no sense, but your servant attacked our guards and had to be subdued. He must pay restitution to the temple before he can go free."

Abram felt as if he had been kicked in the stomach. Abithar had been his man servant for over twenty years. In many ways, he was like family. "And if he is unable to pay such a... price, what then?"

A thin smile played upon the lips of Dumuzid. "Why, then he joins the blessed ranks of those set aside for the next blood moon sacrifice. Our blessed Nanna and her consort Sin will accept his payment... in blood."

"I will appeal to King Ur-Nammu, in this case. He will see fit to execute justice instead of a servant who was only doing his duty.", said Abram.

"Do what you will, Abram, son of Terah, heretic and liar! But know this! Our king does not involve himself in affairs of the temple. He knows his place and it is in governing the Empire, not managing the religions of the state. Two weeks, then it is the time of the blood moon. You have until then to either pay the debt… or let your man pay it himself." Dumuzid turned and walked out of the room, leaving Abram fuming. Abram turned to go, only to find his way blocked by the same burly temple guard he had seen holding Abithar on the steps.

"You'd best find a way to pay the debt, Lord Abram, Ur-Nammu's hands are tied by the loyalty of the populace to Nanna, Queen of the Night. I will escort you out."

Abram hurried to Terah's home, him and Sarai having moved out after their nuptials. He did the customary washing and entered to find Terah, his father, and Nahor, his younger brother, involved in business talk. Quickly, he relayed his exchange with Dumuzid and the temple guard. The color drained from Terah's face when Abram told them of the threat involving Abithar and the blood moon sacrifice.

Terah exclaimed, "I can't believe that the rumors are true…. that Dumuzid has planned to escalate the appeasement of their false goddess from animal to human sacrifice. This must be brought to the attention of Ur-Nammu at once! Abram, come with me! Nahor, if you will, stay and handle the business we were discussing."

As they made their way to the palace, Terah continued, "The priests of Molech have long desired this – the sanction of human sacrifice in our city. I have never spoken of this, my son, for it sickens me to do so; but on my travels, I would come across high places dedicated to Molech still smoldering with the remains of children on the altar! Precious children! I can think of nothing that upsets me more than to think of God's greatest gift to us, allowing us to participate in His creation of life by having children, being abused and burned upon a pagan altar to a fictitious god!" "Promise me you will never do such a thing! Promise me!"

"I promise, father – although I have never seen it with my own eyes, I can think of no greater sin than to kill your own beloved child. I cannot fathom it!", replied Abram.

"If the priests of Nanna condone human sacrifice, then soon the fires of Molech will be emboldened to follow. Whereas Dumuzid would reserve it for special occasions, the priests of Molech would seize the opportunity to institute it regularly into their vile rites." Ur-Nammu must intervene and put a stop to this! If not, then Ur will soon become a place where life is cheap, and the helpless will become fodder for the blood lusts of the wicked.", concluded Terah, as they arrived at the Palace.

The guards showed them quickly in, as Terah was a frequent guest of the king, for he consulted with him on commerce and trade vital to the security of the Empire. Entering the throne room, Ur-Nammu spied Terah and extended his scepter in welcome. First Terah, then Abram, touched their foreheads and then touched the extended scepter in deference and respect to the king.

"To what do I owe this unexpected visit from my trusted advisor and his first born son?", said the king.

"My King, I come with grave news concerning the riot late this morning in the marketplace near the temple of Nanna. My son, Abram, will tell you his firsthand account of these alarming events."

"Yes, a regrettable affair. Fortunately, no blood was spilled. I understood the matter was settled. What is the cause for alarm?"

Abram briefly, but thoroughly, detailed his accounting of the riot in the marketplace earlier that day. He also told of his encounter with Dumuzid when he went back to retrieve his man servant who had been detained by the temple guard.

The king swore. "That meddling charlatan! He's challenging me to a test of power, knowing full well that I must respond or back down. I'm afraid your man is but a small game piece in a much bigger game, Abram… a deadly game, to be sure, but a game it is; of power and influence over the people of Ur."

Terah interjected, "The game is deadlier than you might imagine, my king, if the practice of human sacrifice spreads within the Empire. The priests of Molech would seize this opportunity to sanction the practice everywhere, every temple day. Whereas, now they hide the practice and perform their blood rites in remote places using children of blinded devotees of their barbaric beliefs; when sanctioned by the state religion, no child anywhere would be safe."

"Ur-Nammu pondered these words and turned to his scribe, "Send this message to the temple of Nanna. No, send it to *all* of the temples of all of the gods of Ur, especially Molech, Marduk, An, Nanna, Enlil, and Ninlil.

"By order of the king, due to economic conditions in the Empire, no single temple sacrifice shall exceed the price of a yearling bullock. All sacrifices must come under the inspection of government officials for civil tax purposes. Any sacrifice exceeding the cost of a yearling bullock will constitute a breach of law and will subject the temple to a tax of one hundred *siqlahem* of gold per sacrifice."

Terah chuckled. "I bow to your wisdom, my king – it seems you have learned the lessons of economics well. Hit them in their coffers, and see them back down."

Ur-Nammu nodded, "I have you to thank for this lesson. It has proved to be most effective in dealing with wayward city-states of our Empire. Let's see how it works with the priests, as well. This should stop any human sacrifice, as the value of a human, even a slave or child, far exceeds that of a bullock. A word of caution, Abram, if I may."

"I am your servant, my king.", replied Abram.

"Get your man out of that temple by any means possible. My forces cannot directly assault the temple. It would mean civil war in Ur. I fear the response of the priests when they understand the purpose behind this new law. They may take out their fury upon him, and thus you, for this edict. Act with haste. My forces will look the other way."

The king pressed his cylindrical seal upon the cuneiform tablet which carried the edict, making it law. It would be copied and relayed by courier throughout the land within hours. Abram knew he had little time to rescue Abithar from the hands of soon-to-be angry men.

Chapter 4

Stealth or Strength? That was the question. Terah commanded no small force of guards himself for the caravans he directed. It was a grim necessity against the roving bandits of the deserts of the south and the mountains of the west. Abram decided against an all out assault on the temple, Abithar would likely be dead before they found him if brute force were used. And it might spark another riot, this time with bloodshed. No, surprise was their greatest ally at this point. And he needed information.... details of the temple, places hidden to the common man but known to priests themselves. And he needed it now.

Finding Lot at one of his usual haunts, Abram quickly took him aside and filled him in on the situation. For once, Lot's association with some of the seedier people of Ur proved useful. He found a former temple guard that had been dismissed by the priests over some minor incident who drew them a crude map of the temple interior on a scraped sheepskin with a bit of charcoal. Most importantly, he knew where they were likely keeping the man.

As Abram paid him some ten silver shekels for the information, the former guard remarked, "Watch out for Hirk-uz, the big guard. He's Dumuzid's right hand man and enforcer. He's not only loyal to the chief priest, he's a true believer in Nanna." He spat as he said the name. "I have no love for the temple or its priests. They are a cruel group who exploit their followers for personal gain. I would have gladly helped you without the payment." He hefted the coin purse containing the ten silvers, "But since I have it, I will keep it, it will help keep the wife from harassing me about work for awhile. May you prosper in your endeavor." The guard clasped Lot's forearm and then turned back to his drink.

Abram rolled the map up, tying it with a bit of loose hide. "Let us make haste to the market. We need a diversion, something to occupy the attention of the guards while I slip back to free Abithar and any other poor soul they might have back in the sacrificial stalls. You will need to create a commotion. With the guards on alert from the riot already today, it shouldn't be hard to get something going."

Lot shook his head. "Nay, uncle, it is you that will make the diversion, and I who will free Abithar. You are too well known by the priests to be hidden. I, on the other hand, am virtually unknown to both guards and temple lackeys. I think you should march right up to the side steps and demand to see the chief priest there, in front of the market."

"You may have a point, although I am loathe to admit it. Your plan does have its merits. Are you sure you can find Abithar?" He passed the map to Lot.

"I can. If he is where Tarmon the guard said he should be, and even if he is not. I listened carefully as he drew the map explaining the various parts of the temple and their functions. Abithar may be held in a different section of the temple. But I am fast, and I am young. And…. I am used to fleeing quickly from a sticky situation."

Abram grinned. "Of that, I have no doubt."

Passing Sinbar, the blind beggar, Abram had a sudden thought.   Dropping a coin into his bowl, he knelt and asked a question. "Sinbar, although you are blind in your eyes, you 'see' more than most in this foul city. Is there a secret way into the ziggurat of Nanna?"

Sinbar thanked Abram for the coin. "Oh, most noble Abram, my ears hear things most do not. I knew it was you and your brother, Lot, long before you reached my mat. Your step is distinct upon the clay of Ur, and your generosity has been great through the years. Yes, there is a way. Go, send Lot around to the east side of the temple. Hidden behind a mustard bush is a small entrance used by temple spies to report directly to Dumuzid." He laughed. "Most people do not take notice of a blind beggar, and they assume I must be deaf and dumb too, for they say things as they walk the street that would astound you." He motioned for Abram to come closer and he lowered his voice. "Lord Abram, get your man and leave this city. There is a plot brewing by the priests of all of the temples against you, your father, and your wives, because of your vocal belief in One God. You are not safe in Ur."

Abram took the advice seriously, dropped another coin into Sinbar's bowl and the pair hurried on toward the market with determined steps.

~~<Θ>~~

Abram hugged Lot one last time, cautioning him to be careful. "Give me about a half hour to get Dumuzid's attention. Then slip in the spy door Sinbar told us about. Carry this with you." Abram produced the same crude, short staff from his robe that he had made earlier that day during the riot.

Lot took the impromptu weapon, feeling its weight in his hands. "This ought to even the odds somewhat, uncle! I never knew you were given to clubbing people. Where did you get this?"

"Never mind, just keep it hidden in your robes unless you have to use it. Lot, I'm counting on you to come back safe. Father will kill me if something happens to you. So, be careful!"

Lot smiled. "When have I ever *not* been careful.... strike that, when have I ever *not* been resourceful to escape?"

Abram snorted, "You are quite the slippery one, at that. You were made for intrigue."

The two shared a brief prayer to the Lord God to bless their efforts and parted ways. Abram made his way to the steps of the Ziggurat and demanded to see Dumuzid. The guards indicated that he should follow them. Abram steadfastly refused and demanded that Dumuzid see him there on the steps in front of the market. He called for Hirk-Uz by name, surprising the guards with the information. They hurried to find their burly captain. He emerged from the depths of the temple.

"I hear you are asking to see Dumuzid again. He does not grant audiences twice in one day, especially to heretics.", Hirk-Uz stated.

"If he wants his blood money for my man, then he will meet me on my terms, here and now, in front of the people.", replied Abram.

Startled, Hirk-Uz eyed Abram suspiciously. "You have the payment? Here and now?" Looking around, he said, "Where is it?"

"Do you think I would be foolish enough to bring it here alone? It is close by, I have only to signal and it will be brought to my feet." Abram raised his voice, "Two thousand silver shekels do not fit in a purse you wear on your belt."

A tremor ran through the marketplace. Two thousand silver shekels! Heads turned, and a buzz began as people began drifting toward the scene of the confrontation. Hirk-Uz sent a messenger into the temple. Soon, more temple guards arrived as the crowd began to grow. Noticeably absent were the military guards that Ur-Nammu had stationed around the market to keep the peace. Hirk-Uz must have noticed this too, as his contingent of guards was twice what it had been that morning during the riot. Suddenly, the chief priest Dumuzid appeared.

"I hear you are ready to redeem your man servant for the crimes he committed against the temple this morning.", Dumuzid sneered.

"On one condition, priest.", said Abram.

"Oh, I do not recall any conditions in our conversation earlier; just payment for damages and lost revenue.", huffed Dumuzid.

"That is the condition I am referring to, priest. I give you this money, and you give each and every merchant a portion of that money for *their* lost revenue, for *their* damages, for *their* lost time and merchandise because of the riot this morning."

Dumuzid blanched. He had never intended to give any money to anyone, if it ever was forthcoming. But Abram had outmaneuvered him by publically calling for restitution to the shopkeepers. The crowd began shouting, calling for payment. Abram smiled at the priest, knowing he had just created an unwinnable situation for his opponent. He just hoped this little ruse would give Lot the time he needed to rescue Abithar.

Lot made his way swiftly around the pyramidic structure to the eastern side. Looking around to make sure no one saw him, he ducked behind the shrubbery that lined the base of the temple. Feeling his way along, he found some steps leading to a small wooden door. He took a small knife out, tucked it in his waistband, and then hid his shepherd's satchel in the bushes. The locking thong was out, indicating that a spy was probably on his way to the temple to report. Lot opened the door silently and crept into the empty corridor. The dim light of distant torches made flickering shadows on the wall. Lot closed the door behind him, pulling the locking thong inside the hole which ran through the door. "No unexpected company coming up behind me in the dark.", he thought to himself. Orienting himself to where he was in the temple, Lot made his way south toward the place indicated on their map where the daily temple sacrifices were kept. Just as he feared, only goats and sheep filled the narrow stone stalls. No guards here, only a novice attendant feeding the soon-to-be slaughtered animals. Lot kept hidden in the shadows and made his way silently toward the guard room. "If I were going to keep a prisoner, I would keep him in the most secure place in the temple.", Lot reasoned. "Which gives me a bigger problem, how am I going to subdue a whole room full of guards with just a long club? Oh well, I will have to figure that out when I get there.", he thought. He wiped his sweaty palms on the front of his robe and gripped the short staff tighter.

As he carefully worked his way toward the guard room, it dawned on Lot that he had not seen a single guard since entering the structure. Buoyed by this thought, he ran silently up the narrow corridor toward his destination. "Either these guards are extremely stupid and lazy, or Abram is a better troublemaker than I give him credit.", thought Lot. Rounding a corner, his luck ran out as he ran face to face with two guards escorting Abithar and two other prisoners toward the direction of the sacrificial stalls. It seems Tarmon, the former guard, knew his business better than Lot imagined, only they had waited to move the prisoners to the stalls after a bit of interrogation by the temple inquisitors.

Lot shoved the staff into the first guard's abdomen, knocking his breath from him. He pivoted on his left foot, as the second guard rushed him. Abithar tripped the guard and Lot knocked him out with a blow to the back of the head. He did the same to the first guard who was retching for breath on his knees. It was over in a matter of seconds.

"Hurry! Follow me!", Lot said as he took his small knife and slashed the ropes binding the prisoners. He retraced his steps, avoiding the stalls, and lifted the bar holding the secret door shut. Lot, Abithar, a young boy, and an older man ran, blinking, into the sunlight on the eastern side of the temple. "I must let Abram know we are out!", said Lot. He took a small ram's horn from the leather satchel he had left in the bushes. Raising it to his lips he gave three short blasts, the agreed upon signal that Abithar had been freed. "Go with haste to Terah's home! He is making ready to depart Ur, for this challenge will not go unpunished by the evil minions of the temple of the Moon Goddess." He looked at the man and the young boy he supposed was his son. "You are welcome to join us, or stay and become drink for Dumuzid's thirst for blood."

"If it is all the same, we will join you in your flight from Ur... I am newly here from Damascus. Only let me first get my wife and daughter, we were taken in the night, and she has no knowledge we are alive.", the man stated.

"Make haste! Take only what you can carry on a donkey or mule. We leave at sunset headed northwest along the Great River road.", said Lot.

"I will meet you there. Ur is no place to live, if a man and his son can be stolen in the night by those in power. I have heard of Lord Terah. He is a fair man, perhaps he can use an extra hand with his herds.", the man exclaimed.

Lot motioned for them to go, "I will wait for Abram by the mat of Sinbar, the blind beggar. Abithar, tell Terah all is well, and we will be there shortly."

Abram heard the signal and faced the stormy countenance of Dumuzid, the high priest, with renewed confidence. He pointed his finger at him. "The Lord God of Heaven and Earth, the Creator of all that is, the One True God condemns you for your false ways, priest!" "I will not pay your extortion, nor will my servant die – for you have underestimated the power of the One True God, who has seen fit to undo your plans to sacrifice men on the altar of blood."

The crowd howled in rage at the news that neither would they get the aforementioned payment and the news that the temple had planned to sacrifice humans instead of animals. They stormed the steps of the temple, as Abram turned and stalked away. He heard the guttural scream of his enemy as he hurried away, "You'll pay for this! I swear it, Abram, you'll pay for this!"

Abram made his way to the mat of Sinbar, where he found an amused Lot waiting. "Have a few words with the priest, did you?", said Lot. Abram threw up his hands, "What can I say? Father says I'm not good with words." They clapped each other on the back, dropped another coin in Sinbar's bowl, and made their way quickly home. Behind them, Sinbar took the coin from his bowl and marveled at its value... for it was gold.

Chapter 5

Living In Harran

"Stop fidgeting and hold still!" Sarai clasped Abram's hand tightly as she peered closely for the thorn which had caused him to complain loudly and constantly of its presence in the fleshy part of his thumb. She took her bone needle and probed.

"Ow! Ow! Ow! That hurts!", said Abram, as he snatched his hand back from her grasp, almost causing her lose her balance and fall.

"Honestly, you big baby! Be a man, won't you! Let me get it out!", she said.

"I'll think I'll let it fester first, then it will pop right out.", he said, holding his hand in the other.

"Oh, no you won't... Milpah, fetch the white vinegar from the cooking tent. We are going to take care of this today, Abram, the whole encampment is tired of your complaining and ill temper simply because of a tiny thorn.", said Sarai. Milpah hurried out of the tent. Sarai stared Abram down and held out her hand.

Defeated, Abram gingerly gave his hand back to his wife. Milpah, Sarai's hand maiden, returned; carefully ducking low under the tied flap of the tent, holding a red clay saucer of clear liquid.
"Now, I am going to open the place where the thorn is with this." – holding up her bone needle– "...and then I will pour the vinegar into the opening to float out the thorn. If that does not work, then I will gently squeeze the base of your thumb until the thorn backs out enough for me to catch it between my fingernails." "Do you understand? Am I making myself clear? It *will* hurt a little. But... I will reward you later, if you are good boy for me."

Abram had to laugh. "Wife, I know I have been acting childish – it's only that this thorn seems to be the brick that broke this mule's back today." "Go ahead, I'll be good…. and I will take you up on your promise of a reward, too!" His eyes twinkled as he spoke.

Sarai smiled, lighting up the tent and Abram's world with her beauty. She went right to work and after only a few seconds, she raised her head. "There, it's out! Now wasn't that simple?"

Abram rubbed his hands together with satisfaction. "You are a delight to me, my beloved. What would I do without you? I must return to the shearing tent now, but I will be back later this evening… for my reward!"

Sarai watched him go, her heart filled with love for her man, yet empty with the gnawing fear that she had just experienced the closest thing to motherhood she would ever know.

Abram closed the flap on his and Sarai's tent and surveyed the hillside where the herds had settled. He noted with satisfaction that his chief under-shepherd, Eliezer of Damascus, had moved the main body of sheep further up the mountain to greener pastures. The key to healthy sheep was to keep them moving, not let them stay too long in one place. Overgrazing also hurt the land, as the forage was depleted too fast and took longer to recover. He thought back to how God had brought him to the clan on the day they had left Ur some ten years previously. Lot had rescued him and his son, Isafer, from the temple of Nannu along with Abithar, Abram's own man servant. In gratitude, Eliezer and his family had joined them on their pilgrimage to Harran. He had proved to be a valuable asset, with a quick mind and an easy spirit, who rapidly moved up the ranks of his many shepherds to become his chief under-shepherd. Everyone liked him, too. Even Lot had felt no resentment at Eliezer's promotion. Besides, Lot was busy with the goats, he preferred them to the sheep, anyway.

Abram strapped on his sandals and made haste to the shearing tent where Terah was, no doubt, anxiously waiting. Terah trusted no one else other than Abram to oversee the shearing. Since Terah's vision had clouded somewhat with age, he didn't even trust himself. Their flocks had grown. Terah had continued his trade business, with Cherah managing the textile end of things in town; but the bulk of the family's wealth still lay in the cattle, the goats, and sheep that Terah, Abram, and now Lot, owned and kept in the hills surrounding Harran. Lot had sued for a small herd as wages and Terah had agreed. Lot had also finally settled down somewhat from his waywardness, and was actually courting the daughter of a carpenter from Harran in the proper way. Terah was hoping Lot would marry a relative, but was content as long as she was counted as one of the believers in the One True God. Lot had assured them that she was.

"So many ready to shear!", thought Abram, "It will be long after dusk before we are through." He called for Abithar to bring the lamps and oil that he knew they would need later. "I'll be fortunate to be back at my tent before bedtime.", he thought woefully, recalling his wife's promise. "I should not complain about having too much to do.", he thought, "It could be the other way around, and I not have anything to do; no sheep to shear, nor flocks to watch. God is good." He went right to work.

"Abram! I am the One True God who made both Heaven and Earth! Separate yourself from your father Terah and get thee unto a land that I will show thee. I will make of you a great nation – your name shall be great and all peoples of the earth shall be blessed because of your faith. I will bless those who bless you and curse those who curse you. Hasten to obey the word of your God!"

Abram woke in a sweat with the words still ringing in his mind. The moonlight played upon the features of his lovely wife and he shook her awake."Sarai! Sarai! Wake up! I have been visited by the Lord!", exclaimed an excited Abram to a sleepy Sarai.

She bolted upright, suddenly awake at his words. "What did He say? Husband, did He say anything about a child?"

"Not in so many words, although He did allude to it.", Abram said.

Her disappointment evident, Sarai continued, "Are you sure this was the Lord God and not one of the dream demons of Carchemish trying to confuse or mislead you?"

"No, No! It was *our* God! The God of our fathers, of Terah, and Shem, and Noah!

He spoke to me, Sarai, He spoke to me!"

"Well, tell me what He said then, my husband. You say He 'alluded' to children but didn't actually mention them?"

"Yes, He said he would make my name great, and of me a great nation, and all the peoples of the world would be blessed because of my faith…"

"Did He happen to mention me in any of this?", she inquired.

"Well, no, but you know that God means us both in this; He, after all, brought you to me. Oh, and He also said that we must leave Harran. I must separate from my father and find a land that He will show me."

"What?! Just like that? We pick up and leave your father now? How will he manage without you? He's well advanced in age and can no longer do the things he took for granted even a year ago."

"Yes, he is one hundred and forty-five years old by his own accounting. He has declined much since the passing of mother last year. I must talk to him first thing in the morning, to tell him what God has commanded."

"Tell me again, Abram, exactly what the Lord God said to you in your sleep last night.", asked Terah.

Abram relayed word for word the message burned into his memory that God has spoken to him the previous night.

"And did you see Him? Was there any vision to go with the voice?", continued Terah.

"No…. only a thick smoke, as it is when we offer the burnt sacrifices to God. The rich smell of seared meat and the sweet scent of spices filled the air as the voice thundered around me. I could not pinpoint a location to the voice, it echoed as if in a valley surrounded by mountains.", said Abram, as he struggled to recall the details of everything besides the message itself.

Terah sighed. "It is the Lord…. Bless His Holy Name, although He has never revealed it to me. You must do as He says, and I must gird up my loins and get off my bed of mourning for your mother and see to our livelihood. It seems He is catching two fish with one cast of the net, for I have long felt His displeasure at my idleness."

"Father, I do not want to leave you, but I *know* that this is the voice of the Lord. Sarai asked me if I was sure, and I am… and as surely as He led us to leave Ur to come here, He is leading me to leave here and go…. wherever it is He wants me to go…."

"I know, son, I know." "You have a current tally of your flocks and herds? You know which are yours, which are mine, and which are Lot's, I'm sure. Speaking of Lot, have you told him yet? Do you think he will stay here, now that he is married to Ziphah, the carpenter's daughter?"

"I have not told him yet, my father… only you and Sarai know of this. I will leave the decision up to him whether he goes or stays. We must send word to Nahor in Ur, as well, on the next caravan. It may affect him, as Sarai is the family weaver since mother died."

"Her cloth is only a small change from the fine quality that Cherah produced. It will be missed in the trade. But others have been trained on Nahor's loom, and can make similar styles to advance the business.", Terah concluded. "It was good to see him and his son Iscah last year when they came to help us mourn your mother."

"Sarai will be trading her days at the cotton loom for a goat hair spindle instead, as we will need many tents for herdsmen and their families in the coming days." "There is so much to this I don't know, father. It seems strange to divide the clan and uproot the family merely on the words of a dream. It was so much easier when we moved from Ur. It was clear that we needed to get out before something bad happened. But living here in Harran these past twenty-five years, we've been blessed beyond measure…. I know I have no son, and neither does Lot, but there is still time for that… although Sarai grieves daily over her barrenness."

Terah shrugged. "Perhaps this is what God intends… to show Himself mighty to bring about a Godly nation from you and her in this land He has promised to lead you to. He is the Lord. Let Him do what is right in His sight."

"Selah! May it be so!", said Abram.

~~<Θ>~~

"South? Are you sure He wants us to go south? I hear there are giants down there.", said Lot to Abram.

"I am sure, Lot, the Lord spoke to me again last night and told me to travel toward Shechem, to look for the terebinth trees and pitch our camp under them.", replied Abram.

"All right, Abram, south it is… to the trees, and giants, and whatever else that faces us…", said Lot. "To be honest, I am glad for the move. Ziphah wants me to give up the life of a shepherd and go to Harran and learn carpentry from her father. Honestly, carpentry… can you think of anything less interesting?"

Abram nodded, "Yes, yes, I can. Herding goats!", he deadpanned.

Lot laughed. "You don't mean that! Why, goats are interesting. They make a lot of noise, they butt heads, and they eat just about anything… say, sounds a lot like me."

"Glad to know you know it. No, all joking aside, is Ziphah happy now? Has she reconciled to leaving home?"

"I don't know that she will ever get used to living in a tent, Abram. Sarai has taken to it like a fish to water, but Ziphah likes the city life. She is used to a roof over her head and a well nearby. But she loves me… and… she is pregnant! I've wanted to tell you before now, but I was concerned that it might make Sarai…sad."

Abram tried to hide the pain in his heart as he clasped his nephew to his bosom. "Congratulations, brother! The next generation of Shem; I'm proud for you…. how long until the baby comes?"

"She has missed three cycles, so... maybe six more full moons?", he guessed. "That would bring the child into the world before winter. May it be a son."

"Selah! Perhaps God will bring us both a son in the Promised Land, and heal this aching void in Sarai's life."

"Just Sarai? I have seen how you look at the children of the herdsmen. You love each and every one of them, Abram. You take special time to teach each one of them things a father should teach their own child. You not only want a son, you *need* a son."

Abram grimly agreed. "You are right.", as he folded his arms together, "I desire a child, any man would. As it is, Eliezar stands to inherit the flocks, according to tribal law. He is a good man, but I have not embarked upon this great adventure for the sake of Eliezer. God has promised me that He will bless me, Lot, and I have all I need right now... except a son and heir."

Chapter 6

Living in Canaan Land

Sarai hoisted the water jug onto her hip and made to take the short walk to the stream to get enough for their daily needs. She could have easily sent her hand maiden, Milpah, to do this burdensome task, but she rather enjoyed the break from the spindle and the tents and the little bit of exercise it afforded her. Besides, Milpah was busy helping with the preparation of the noon meal. Abram had declared a holiday, for they had finished setting up the new campsite at Shechem. There were mountains to the north of them and green valleys to the south spreading out from the River Jordan to the Great Sea. There was plenty of room for the flocks, which numbered in the thousands now. Shechem was located on the main trade route to Egypt and afforded some measure of civilization for poor Ziphah, who took badly to the nomadic life of a herder's wife. Sarai had thrown herself into helping Ziphah through her pregnancy; doting on her every need, as if by helping Ziphah give birth, she had some part to play in the child's future. And Ziphah needed her help. She was bigger than she should be and the clan's midwife suspected that Ziphah might be carrying twins. They would know soon. Lot had agreed that Zilphah and he would separate themselves from the main group and pitch their tent closer to the town, so that the birthing could be held in privacy. Sarai had convinced Abram that she should also be allowed to stay close by with her hand maiden so that she could aid the midwife at the appropriate time. Abram wanted nothing more than for her to be happy; so he declared a feast for the evening, and tomorrow, Sarai and Milpah would depart to keep vigil over Ziphah until the child was born.

Sarai kept to the tents for the most part. Her fair skin did not do well in the sun, so she covered her face completely as she left the tent. As she reached the stream, she noticed a plume of dust in the air rising from beyond the trees. Four men on horseback appeared and came swiftly toward the stream. Trying not to show alarm, Sarai continued doing what she was doing and fill her water pot.

"You there! Woman, whose tents are these?", said one of the men as they dismounted and led their horses to drink.

"They are the tents of Abram, my Lord; he is a prophet of the Most High God.", she replied, "And, my husband, I might add."

Showing surprise at her calm demeanor, the man pondered for a moment. "I have heard of this Abram. News of his journey has preceded him along the caravan route. Your people are from Harran, are they not?", he asked.

"Yes… and No… originally my Lord was from Ur, but has lived in Harran for much of his life.", she replied.

"You do not sound as if you are from Ur, woman. Where are you from?", he demanded.

"I grew up near the Chabur River, in the north.", she answered, "south and east of Harran."

Satisfied, he turned to go. Looking back, he made one final remark. "Tell your Lord that this land is occupied by the Canaanites. We, too, have herds that move from place to place. If he wishes to avoid conflict, he may want to move on." With that said, the unnamed horseman mounted his horse and galloped off, leaving Sarai with her heart pounding, shaken in her close encounter with unknown men. She hurriedly filled her water pot and carried it home.

~~<⊖>~~

"How did he sound, Sarai?", Abram inquired. "Was he hostile in any way?"

"No, he just wanted to know who we were.", she answered. "It seems our pilgrimage has raised the attention level of the locals."

"That's understandable. His words might have been a friendly warning, but I am not taking any chances. He might have been a scout for a larger group on the way. We cannot leave now. This is where God told me to come, and this is where we will stay until such time as He tells me to move. I must double the guards." He turned and gave the order to a servant, "See to it that no women venture outside the encampment alone.", ordered Abram. "I will post guards at your tent near Lot's dwelling."

"Won't this make you shorthanded with the flocks?", she asked.

"No, I've had a special force of men training in arms for such as this. I knew we would meet up with someone along the way who would oppose us. They each have a staff, a bronze short sword, and a small copper knife. Some of them are skilled in the slinging of stones. It's time to put their training to use.", said Abram.

Chapter 7

The sound of crying split the air as the midwife pulled the child forth from beneath the birthing stool. She cut the umbilical cord with a flint knife and tied it with a small cord made from goat hair. "You have a daughter, Ziphah, and she is healthy. Just listen to those lungs! I suspect they can hear her over at the main encampment." "Wait! You are not through, girl, there *is* another!" She handed the first child over to Sarai who washed the child in warmed water and wrapped her in a soft blanket. She held the child and waited while the midwife finished the birthing of the second infant. "Another girl, Ziphah. They look to be same twins!" She finished up and Ziphah lay on her pallet while Sarai handed the first baby to Milpah while she cleaned up the second child. "Make sure and mark this child, as she opened the womb and is the firstborn.", Sarai instructed her hand maiden. "If they, indeed, turn out to be same twins – it will be important to know which is which." Milpah took some dye from a small pot near the fire and gently placed a bright red dot on the child's forehead. Ziphah reached gratefully for her babies and began coaxing them to suckle. "Two girls! Lot will be disappointed that at least one is not a boy, but I am satisfied. We have plenty of men, as it is. We needed some more women in this camp!", she remarked. The women nodded in agreement, as it did seem that the boys far outnumbered the girls in recent births among Abram's and Lot's men.

"What shall you name them?", Sarai asked softly. "Oh, I'll wait for Lot to arrive and we will decide together. He should be here soon. He has been counting on a boy, so we haven't thought much on girl names.", Ziphah said.

"Well, you both had better start thinking, for you have two names to come up with, not just one!", Sarai pointed out.

"What are you doing, husband?", asked Sarai.

"Oh, just an idea I had. I am working on some symbols that represent speech and actions, much like the cuneiform writing I grew up with in Ur, only with a simpler text and much fewer symbols.", said Abram. "If this works like I hope it will, we will teach them to the adults and children and be able to record the history of our people, send messages between our herders, and preserve the words from the One True God." "I have been experimenting with different types of writing instruments made from fired reeds dipped in lamp oil mixed with soot. It does not work well with clay, so I have settled on cut sections of leather or scraped sheepskin cured in lime water. It is not perfect, but it will have to do for now."

Sarai stared at her husband. "You never cease to amaze me, Abram. Father Terah was right, you are quite intelligent. Can you show me?"

"Abram! Abram! I will give this land of promise unto your children and your children's children. Now, leave Shechem and travel south and east and camp near to the city of Ai. There, erect an altar to me and make sacrifice to me for your sins, and the sins of your people."

Abram shook Sarai awake once more. "He has spoken to me again, my princess. This time he has said we will have children and this land will be theirs. My sweet, we must move south once again with our people and all that we have."

Sarai's eyes filled with tears. "Children, you say? He said we would have children?"

Abram nodded. They kissed one another as she said huskily, "Well, then we'd better be at the business of making that promise come true." Abram smiled and took her in his arms.

Abram ordered the move the next morning. God's timing was perfect, as the flocks needed to graze beyond the hills where they had stayed through the winter. He was worried about the lateness of the spring rains. If the rains did not come soon, all of the livestock would suffer. It was good that God was telling them to travel east toward the Jordan, although the land there more settled than the area to the west, the fields would be green longer nearer the river. The way was mostly south, however, and Abram longed for the temperate climates promised by a lower elevation. The winter snows in Mt. Hermon ought to melt giving a spring run-off in just a few weeks. All in all, trusting God was working out perfectly.

Chapter 8

Abram carried the stones himself to the top of the hill between Bethel and Ai. He stacked the uncut stones one upon the other to make a crude table on which to work. Then he took a lamb, one he himself had inspected to make sure that it was flawless. "Only the best for the Lord God.", he thought. Eliezer accompanied him, carrying the wood for the burnt offering. Swiftly he worked, slicing the throat of the lamb with a quick motion and catching the blood in a clay basin he had brought just for this action. He poured the blood upon the altar and then placed wood on top of the blood. He then positioned the lamb directly in the center of the woodpile and took the torch from Eliezar and placed it under the wood. Finally, he took the spiced oil that Sarai had prepared and cast it upon the tiny flame, which flared to life and filled the hillside with the mingled smell of sacrifice.

He then spoke in a loud voice, "Lord God of Heaven and Earth, You who have made yourself known unto men, the One True God of my fathers. You have revealed Yourself unto me and granted me Your promise of blessing, and honor, and a heritage in this land. Blessed be Your Name, O Creator God! Turn now Your wrath from us, O Lord, accept this sacrifice of blood for the sins of Thy servants. As You did this for our fathers, may You also do this for us, that we may live."

Eliezer quietly surveyed the scene as the fire crackled and the flames leapt into the darkening sky. Abram bowed his head and fell to his knees and smote his breast. After a few moments of silence, Abram stood up and turned to go. "Come, Eliezer, let us go and trust God to honor His word."

The pair left the hillside to make their way back to camp, as the fire slowly died down to glowing embers in the night. Only the sound of the wind rustling in the tall grass of the hilltop remained.

"We cannot stay in Canaan any longer, Abram. The sheep are dying, and the cattle have grown thin. If we head south now, we might just save half of them by the time we reach the Nile. I hear that the drought has not affected Egypt.", said Eliezar. Lot nodded in agreement. Abram had steadfastly refused to move from Bethel until he had another vision from God.

"God has been faithful to let us know when to move, my friends.", said Abram. "I fear to get ahead of God and make such a decision without His voice guiding me."
Eliezar turned to go, obvious in his disagreement with Abram's decision.

Lot lingered and said, "Abram, I have followed you from Ur to Harran, from Harran to Shechem, and now from Shechem to Bethel. I trust you to do the right thing. Only, ask Sarai what she thinks about a sojourn in Egypt. Only until the rains come and the grass grows once again here in the Land of Promise. I do not know why He withholds the rain. You followed His instructions completely. You built His altar, you offered the sacrifice without spot or blemish unto Him, and yet.... it has been over a year since it rained. The Jordan is so weak that you can ford it anywhere. There simply isn't anyplace left for the flocks to graze. Eliezar is right. We would be fortunate to save half of the animals if we left today. Perhaps this is God's way of telling us to move. Will you talk to Sarai about it?"

Begrudgingly, Abram agreed. He knelt in prayer once again to the God of the Heavens and begged Him once more to send rain upon the earth.

"It's not like you to be afraid, my husband. You have always seemed so self assured of every decision.", clucked Sarai. "We have discussed this and I think that Lot is right."

"I know, I know, only I keep remembering stories of Egypt from the caravan drivers my father employed when we lived in Ur. They told us tales of the absolute power of the Pharoah over life and death. Some even worship him as a God. I have had enough of pagan ways! I do not want to travel to such a place where they throw infants into the Nile to appease their Crocodile God.", he snorted. "One other memory makes me hesitant, as well.", whispered Abram.

"Oh? What could scare you more than the crocodiles of the Nile?", Sarai mused.

"The caravan drivers used to tell us how.... ugly... all the women are in Egypt – dark, squat, short women with faces that would make a jackal howl."

Sarai burst into uncontrolled laughter. It was several moments before she could stop, wiping the tears of mirth from her eyes.

"It's not funny, wife! I am afraid because of you... because you are so beautiful that I fear that they will want you for themselves.... and that they will kill me to get you."

Sarai stopped laughing suddenly. "You're serious, aren't you? You really think that I am more desirable than a queen of the Nile? How sweet! My darling husband, I love you so. Let us not stop loving each other ever, my Abram."
"What would you have me do?"

"I will agree to this move on one condition; that we hide your status as my wife from the Egyptians and tell them that you are my sister. It is not really a lie. It is only... not... the whole truth. This way, they will not kill me to get you."

"I don't like it, Abram. It is deceptive. I have never known you to be anything but completely honest in all your dealings."

"Princess, these are my terms for the move. I have not heard from God in this, and I have thought this through. Perhaps we can stay just awhile in Egypt until the rains come here in the north without them ever knowing of your beauty. Keep to the tents and wear your shawl as a veil when you go out. I will not go otherwise."

"May it be as you wish, my Lord. Let us tell Lot and Eliezar to start packing the tents!", said Sarai.

Chapter 9

In and Out of Egypt

The people of Abram, now being called Hebrews by the Canaanites, made their way south toward Egypt; across the Sinai desert, and into the land of Goshen. Just as Eliezar had predicted, they arrived with only half of their flocks still intact. They settled into the Nile delta area near Goshen. Just before they arrived, Abram took Sarai aside for a final talk.

"Remember our agreement, Sarai, you are to stay hidden away as much as possible; and you are to keep your status as my wife a secret from the Egyptians.", warned Abram.

"As you wish, my husb... my brother. If we are to keep up this ruse, we must separate to different tents. I still don't like it, though... it feels... wrong.", said Sarai.

"The Egyptians are a superstitious people, Sarai. They have a god for everything, just like back in Ur. I do not trust them. Father Terah had many trades go sour with the Egyptians for there are few of them that know what it means to have honor and to deal justly. They see what they want and they take it; and I fear that attitude comes from the highest ruler in the land on down. If Pharoah hears of you and your great beauty, they will come for you. I'm sure of it."

"I trust you, Abram. We will do as you see fit. Everyone in the whole camp must be made aware of this, however, or else your plan will come to naught. If they suspect you are hiding the truth, they just might kill all of us."

"God will protect us. He has promised that He will make of my descendents a great nation and that all the people of the world will be blessed. How can that happen if we are all dead? No, dear sister, we will survive Egypt."

For several months things went well. The Egyptians tolerated the refugees, for they had come with things of value to trade; and they had gold and silver, as well, with which to buy. One morning, Sarai had to fetch water from the well instead of Milpah, who was ill with a fever. She was careful to wrap her shawl around not only her head, but the lower part of her face, as well. Only her emerald green eyes were left showing. She hefted the water pot onto her hip and made her way down the narrow path to stand in line and wait her turn to draw water.

Abram happened to be away trading some of their cattle in Memphis in exchange for corn. They had heard rumors that the famine was abating in Canaan, but Abram wanted to have enough feed for both his people and his livestock before making the journey back north.

As Sarai waited her turn at the well, people began walking past; first a few, then more and more, as if they were in a hurry to go somewhere. Sarai overhead some of the women remark that they had heard that two of Pharoah's own sons were coming this way in their chariots, on their way back from the Great Sea where they were inspecting ships for Pharoah. The people were anxious to leave the well, for they were sure to stop and water their steeds there. Sarai almost left and went back to her tent, but she knew that if she left her place, it would be hours before she could come again, so she stayed. It proved to be the wrong decision. No sooner had she moved to her turn at the well than down the road came a string of men on horseback and two chariots being pulled by white horses. The people fell prostrate as the chariots passed them. Sarai did not. The woman who had tried for so long to remain inconspicuous had suddenly become the most conspicuous person in Goshen.

A slim man with a shaven head leapt from his horse and rushed to strike Sarai for her lack of respect for the princes of Egypt.

"Hold! Do not strike her, Kel-sop-rah. I wish to speak with her!", came a shout from one of the chariots.

"My Lord!", said the guard, who fell prostrate before the richly dressed young man who stepped down from his chariot and advanced on the two.

The prince studied the lithe figure of Sarai for moment. "I'm curious, why did you not fall down as the others do, woman with the emerald eyes?", he asked.

She lowered her gaze and stared at his feet, "Because I am a sojourner in this land, my Lord; and I know not the customs of this place. I am one of the Hebrews, the sister of Abram, our leader. We are followers of the One True God, who bids us to bow only to Him."

"How quaint! One God, you say? What a novel idea! I have not heard of this belief before. Your leader... Abram, you say? He is your brother? Are you ashamed to be seen? Why are you so wrapped up on such a hot day? Come, take off your shawl so that I may see what a 'Hebrew woman' looks like."

"I'd rather not, Lord....?"

"Mentuhotep, I am the eldest son of Pharoah, who is also named Mentuhotep. I will rule this land one day. Do not test my patience, woman.... I would see who I am talking to."

Sarai slowly unwrapped her shawl from her face and lifted her eyes to see the startled gaze of the young prince. She could see already that Abram's worst fears were being realized, for she saw desire fill his eyes.

"Well, I must say, that Hebrew women are quite lovely. My compliments to your parents for producing not only a leader of men; but a very desirable daughter, as well. My father is currently on his way north by barge from Thebes to Memphis to consult with me and my brother. I'm sure he would like to meet one of his newest subjects, especially the sister of the leader of the Hebrews.". said the young prince.

Sarai was trapped. One did not refuse an invitation to meet a king, especially when issued by his eldest son. "I await your command, Lord Mentuhotep.", she replied.

"See, Kel-sop-rah? You do not have to beat a woman to get her to respect you, only talk reasonably to her, and she will see the error of her ways."

"Yes, my prince. Thank you, my prince.", he genuflected.

Turning back to Sarai, he asked, "Oh! And when we send for you, whom shall we send for, sister of Abram, leader of the Hebrews? What is your name?"

"My name is Sarai.", she replied.

Chapter 10

Abram turned to go from Pharoah's grainery in Memphis, satisfied with his deal for enough corn, barley, and wheat for his people to make the trek back across the Sinai to Bethel. Lot was busy making the arrangements for the delivery of the load to their encampment in Goshen when a message arrived for Abram to make haste and return to the tents, that there was problem. He and Lot hurried back to the encampment where a crowd had gathered around Sarai's tent. Alarmed, Abram rushed to see what was the matter, ducking into the tent. Sarai was distraught, for in her absence, Milpah's fever had worsened. Moans and sounds of thrashing were coming from the behind the makeshift curtain that separated Sarai's living quarters from Milpah's. Quiet fell over the tent as Abram entered and Sarai rushed to him.

"Abram, please...you must do something! Pray to the Lord God that Milpah be healed! I need her now more than ever. She has gone into convulsions, and I fear that she will soon die!", lamented Sarai.

"Abram placed a reassuring hand on his wife's arm and said, "Lead me to her."

Sarai and Abram went behind the curtain to the pallet where Milpah lay. For the moment, her convulsions had ceased and she had fallen into a coma, with shallow, ragged, breathing. Abram could not believe how quickly she had deteriorated. Just the day before, Milpah had complained at the noon meal of pain in her side and last evening had taken to her bed with fever. Sarai had brewed some root tea and spoon-fed it to her through the night to help the fever to go down. It had not worked.

"There's more I must tell you, Abram, but not now. Let us concern ourselves with Milpah's recovery right now. Please, husband, let us pray to our God to spare her and raise her from the bed of affliction!"

"We shall, dear wife, we shall. Let us join hands over her and ask the Lord's blessings upon her.", said Abram. Sarai knelt on one side of the pallet and Abram on the other and they clasped hands together over Milpah's prone body and Abram prayed, "Lord God of Heaven and Earth, you who made all there is and ever will be. We ask you to hear our prayer for our servant, Milpah. May you see fit to heal her according to thy tender mercies. Renew her strength, O Lord, and raise her from the bed of sickness. We worship you and give you praise, God of our father. That it might be known in Egypt that there is a God who can heal, may it be done. Selah! "

As Abram prayed, Milpah let out a long slow breath and never took another.

For long minutes, Sarai and Abram remained kneeling beside the pallet holding hands. This was their first physical contact in many months, and they were loathe to let go. Finally, Sarai noticed that Milpah had died and began to sob quietly. Abram said, "He is the Lord, let Him do as He sees fit." Sarai rose and covered the body with a thin linen cloth. She was strangely quiet as she went about the business of gathering things up and cleaning the tent. Abram was puzzled, and grabbed Sarai by the arm as she walked by, her arms laden with Milpah's things.

"Sarai, you must understand… our God cannot be commanded, only asked. And sometimes He says, 'No.'", said Abram softly.

"No, husband, it is *you* that do not understand. Our God has put us to the test, and we have failed. We should have never come to Egypt. The trial is upon us, husband. Pharoah has heard of me and will send for me shortly, just as you feared. I cannot fathom going through what I am about to go through without Milpah at my side; but as you said, 'He is the Lord, let Him do as He sees fit.'", she said bitterly.

Abram swayed and buckled to his knees. "Oh, Sarai! Sarai! I'm so sorry. Would to God that I could turn back the sun and moon and retrace our steps to Canaan!

We must pray again, dear wife, we must pray that God will keep you safe and free from the designs of evil men!"

Sarai spoke not a word, but turned and left the tent to make the announcement that Milpah had died. The sound of mourning rose from the fellow servants outside, for one their own was gone. Abram remained on his knees in the tent, tears pooling in the dust.

~~<⊖>~~

"You have found favor with Pharoah, Lord Abram. He has ordered the royal steward to furnish you with one hundred head of sheep, fifty head of oxen, twenty donkeys, thirty she-asses, twenty camels, and ten servants, male and female. Your sister has made quite the impression on the royal family. She is not only beautiful, she handles herself with poise and grace befitting a queen or consort. You should be proud.", the Viceroy of Memphis hinted boldly.

"Your grace does me honor with this news. I am concerned, however, that my sister is not ready for the courts of Egypt. She is, after all, only a nomadic sheepherder's sister.", said Abram.

"Nonsense! Pharoah has already seen fit to assign to her a royal handmaiden to instruct her in the ways of Egypt. Hagar is one of our best. She will make Sarai to know the customs and ways of our people. She, too, is a rare beauty. Seeing the two together is like seeing a rich mountain next to a clear lake. They are different and yet, both stunning in their own way. Count yourself blessed among men, Abram, for this bounty.", said the Egyptian noble.

"I do, my Lord, I am most blessed.", said Abram through clenched teeth, "When can I see my sister? I have much to talk to her about."

"Oh, come round to the Governor's palace tomorrow where Pharoah and his sons are residing for the season before returning to Thebes. I will let them know you are coming. Have no fear, Abram, all is well. The only question that remains is who will prevail in their bid for her. If the father wants her enough; then, of course, she will be his, for he is Pharoah. But the son is quite taken with Sarai and is suing passionately for her to be given to him. The father might just give in to his son's wishes in this matter. For Sarai, nothing could be better, for her future is assured regardless." The Viceroy smiled in genuine pleasure for the good news he thought he was sharing with Abram.

~~<Θ>~~

Abram showed up at the Governor's palace the next morning and was ushered into Sarai's suite. He asked for and was granted time to be alone with his sister to pray.

"We have little time, Sarai, for you are wanted by both father and son, and these things are settled suddenly in most cases. We will be the last to know, and you will be on your way to the harem of either Pharoah or the Prince before we know the decision has been made.", said Abram."What can we do, Abram? I will not bed another man. I would die first before I allow that to happen. I have confided in Hagar that I am already a married woman and she is sympathetic to our plight. She has no love lost for the Egyptian court, as they have passed her over and made her into my servant. She had high hopes of being the Prince's consort herself once, but now wants nothing more than to escape the country with us, if we leave.", said Sarai.

"Not 'if', but 'when', Sarai.", Abram quipped, "God will not forsake us in this God forsaken land."

"Sarah giggled, "Did you hear what you just said? Oh Abram, I believe you are right. No matter how bleak things seem, God will take care of us. I never told you this; but before I met you, when I was on my way to Ur from my home up north, I despaired of life more than once. I was hungry, tired, and had no money for the journey. More than once I was offered food, lodging, and money by men in exchange for ...... favors. I refused, for I knew God had something greater for me. I believe he still does, my husband. He rescued me from the pit of my despair and the desires of evil men and I believe He will again."

Abram took Sarai by the hand and kissed it. "We will find a way, my princess. God will make it so."

Chapter 11

The next morning, the sun rose upon the Nile River near Memphis with a golden glow. The flood markers had indicated an ideal rise in the Nile for the coming growing season. Everything looked to be a perfect day in the most fertile area of the Nile River Delta. The flood waters had ebbed leaving the deposits of enriched alluvial soil for the raising of crops. Even the insects were co-operating, no locusts or stinging flies had appeared from the red lands – as the Egyptians called the desert - to plague the workers who sowed the seeds for a coming harvest. Huge barges were poled up and down the Nile, sending produce, fruits, and goods throughout the country.

Suddenly, without warning, all of the Egyptians began to have great blisters form on their hands. Even those with calloused hands were affected. No one could do anything. From Pharoah to the most common field worker, every man had great painful blisters on the palms of their hands. Pharoah consulted with his advisors, who interpreted this as a great plague because of a great offense to the gods. But what was the nature of the offense? No one could tell. News of the great plague reached the ears of Abram, who gave praise to God for His Divine intervention. He hurried to tell Eliezar and Lot to spread the news for the Hebrew people to be ready to move. He sat down under an oak tree and waited to hear from Pharoah.

"What do you mean you are married? I understood that Abram was your brother, not your husband! Why have you deceived us thusly?", Pharoah thundered to Sarai; when she, emboldened by the plague, told him of her true status as the wife of Abram. "Send for Abram!", cried Menuhotep to his Viceroy, " Tell him to come at once!"

The Viceroy paled at the words of his king, but left quickly to seek out Abram. His way was impeded by the fact that his chariot driver's hands were bleeding from the painful blisters that had become great sores from holding the reins. The Viceroy had to drive himself toward Goshen. He found him sitting carelessly beneath an oak tree near his tent, calmly fashioning a rope from goat's hair, as if he had not a care in the world. The Viceroy rode up and sputtered, "You have your nerve, shepherd! Pharoah has found out your deception and demands to see you. You had better come at once, or else it will go badly for your sister and your people. Climb aboard my chariot and I will take you to him!"

Abram calmly locked his rope knot into place before looking at the Viceroy, who was getting redder in the face with each passing moment. "What deception are you referring to, my Lord?", asked Abram simply.

"Why the fact that Sarai is not your sister but your wife, you trickster! You cannot deny it, she has already confessed!"

"I do not deny that she is my wife, Viceroy, but you are mistaken in your assumption that I lied to Pharoah. You see; Sarai is my half-sister, the daughter of my father, but not of my mother. Surely you can see that it is Pharoah and his household who have misjudged the situation.", replied Abram.

"I see... I see that you are very good at splitting hairs to your advantage, deceiver! Pharoah is convinced that the plague is a punishment from the heavens for his attempt to lay claim to a married woman, your woman!"

"It's likely that he is correct, for our God is the One True God who made heaven and earth and all that is in it. He controls everything and can certainly bring a plague of blisters without a problem.", said Abram.

Chagrinned at these words, the Viceroy then said, "Let us make haste to Memphis and consult with Pharoah." He swallowed and said quietly, " We will get there faster if you will drive, for I cannot control the reins well." He held out his hands to show them red and swollen from the painful blisters that infected them.

"Take your sister and leave our lands! Take all of the gifts I gave you, as well! Ask your God to take with Him also the great plague He visited upon my people!", said Pharoah to Abram.

"As you wish, Lord Mentuhotep. We will leave as soon as our tents are struck.", replied Abram.

"One last question, Abram. Why would you do this? Why would you come into our land and hide your wife in such a manner? What if I had taken her to my bed? Why would you risk such a thing and bring shame to your house and death to mine?"

For the first time, Abram faltered. He seemed much embarrassed as he replied, "Oh Pharoah, it is my first time in Egypt, yet I heard from my youth in my father's house tales of the absolute power of the Pharoah in Egypt. You have seen my wife, yet you know not the half of her value. It would surprise you to know this, we were married over thirty –five years ago, and yet her beauty has not faded one whit. She is a woman of sixty-five years and yet she looks to be half of that. I feared exactly what came to pass – that you would covet what I had and that you would kill me to get her. Only now, my God has demonstrated His Mighty Hand and brought us out of your power and the power of your Empire, for not a one of your soldiers can draw a sword or pull a bow. We will leave this land, and God willing, we will never come back." Pharoah listened intently to Abram's answer and nodded thoughtfully. "The sons of Abraham may one day return to Egypt; for we are not as dependent on the rains from heaven as the countries surrounding us due to the gift of the Nile. When they do, they will know the wrath of a Pharoah that spares you this day."

"I rather doubt it, Lord Mentuhotep, for you see…. I have no sons." With those words, Abram turned and walked away.

Chapter 12

Looking for a City

The return trip to the hill country of Canaan near Bethel was subdued, but uneventful. It was as if an animal had escaped a trap by gnawing off its foot, yet gripped the bait that had lured it there. They were grateful for the food and the riches that Egypt had supplied to booster the herds and expand the wealth of Abram, yet they were smarting from the loss of Milpah and others they had buried in the rich, dark soil of Egypt. And Sarai was frightened by her near encounter with disaster in Memphis. She often woke up moaning from horrid dreams of Pharoah's painted face hovering above her, about to take her as his own. She had changed in Egypt. Her playful attitude had deepened into a melancholic stupor, which was only exacerbated by the daily reminder of her ordeal in the presence of her handmaiden of Egypt, Hagar. She loved Hagar, however, and had it not been for her friendship, she would have surely lost her mind. It was not her fault that Sarai had almost become the plaything of

Pharoah, but she still could not help but think of her Egyptian trials every time she saw her.

One morning as they approached the place where they had encamped prior to their departure to Egypt the year before, Abram took Sarai aside and said, "Look, wife, we are almost home; back to the land of promise that God gave to us. Let us rejoice and be glad! Put off this spirit of heaviness that weighs you down, for it infects the whole camp. We have left Egypt behind us, let us leave it behind completely! Pharoah cannot get at us here. We are safe... *you* are safe..."

"Oh, Abram, I know what you say is true. Your dreams tell us that God will protect us, and I know He *has* protected us; if only I could make my feelings to feel what my mind knows and my ears hear from your lips. But it is hard, husband, it is so hard. My dreams are of bondage and servitude to a man who is not my husband. My dreams are nightmares that tell me that my beauty is a curse, not a blessing! My fears are that this will happen again! My nights are filled with pain and my days are filled with the reminder of my folly in convincing you to go to Egypt every time I see Hagar."

"Would you have me send her away? I will, if it would comfort you.", said Abram.

"No! Oh no, my dear husband. Although she is a daily reminder of my trials, she has become as much a part of my life as poor Milpah used to be. She is a comfort to me and a great help. I could not do without her. And where would she go? She cannot return to Egypt, for they would take out their wrath upon her for our spoils of their land. No, Abram, do not send her away."

"As you wish, my love. Only, I long to see your smile again, to hear your laughter fill the tents as it used to do.", said Abram tenderly.

"Give me time, Abram, give me time. As the waters of a stream smooth the edges of the roughest rocks, so time will take away the edges of pain and sadness from my heart. You will hear me laugh again, and see me smile, and all the world will remember me; not for being sad, but for my joy!"

Ziphah was unhappy. She had enjoyed their stay in Egypt near the northern city of Memphis. She had even convinced Lot to rent her a house near the outskirts of the city where she and the twins could stay. She so enjoyed her daily walks to the market while her servants minded the children. She loved the city life. She had been raised in Harran and still found the tent life of her husband's people to be cumbersome, hard, and sometimes, lonely. Lot would stay in the fields with the various flocks for days at a time, while she had only her girls to talk to, and they could not yet talk back. And now they were on their way back to camp between Ai and Bethel. These two towns were so small they could hardly be called towns! No, she longed for the city and secretly hoped that she could convince Lot to find one where she could live as she wanted.

Lot counted his flocks of goats and sheep with satisfaction. He thought he had nearly as many as Abram. The year spent in Egypt had done wonders for the flocks who multiplied rapidly in the tropical paradise of the Nile delta. And the fact that Abram had shared some of the sheep that Pharoah had given him did not hurt either. They needed new blood infused into the herd from time to time to keep the sheep from growing weak with the wasting disease. Gone were his early years of mischievous jaunts and shirking of his duties. Lot had to hand it to Terah who had, despite Lot's nature otherwise, infused Lot with a sense of duty to family. He thought about his wife and daughters. "I want my girls to grow up and marry well. I want them to have strong husbands who fear God and work hard, like their father, and his father before him – strike that, his grandfather...", Lot thought to himself. "God is good. He has given to me a wife and two daughters and I know he will give me sons, as well.", thought Lot. "Ziphah will bear me sons, just as she bore me my girls. I have only to be patient, as Abram has patiently waited on Sarai all these years. Poor Sarai, she is no longer young, although she still looks it. I wonder if the way of women still visits her each moon? Perhaps Ziphah knows... I will have to ask her sometime.", he mused. Lot finalized his tally, a broad smile spreading across his face at the total.

Abram was busy teaching one of the children how to hold the reed quill at the proper angle to get the right amount of ink to flow upon the papyrus parchment that Abram had learned of while in Egypt. Abram had made arrangements for the buying of it from the caravans which traveled up and down the route from Egypt to Damascus. "Careful! The paper is thin and soaks up the ink quickly! You must keep moving to make the marks like so… from right to left." Abram demonstrated again for the young boy named Baruch how to write the symbols.

"It's not fair… it's easier for you… you write with your left hand and can make the symbols without smearing them with the heel of your palm.", Baruch muttered as he lifted his hand to demonstrate the black ink on the edge of his right hand. Abram laughed. "I never thought of that when I decided to simplify the symbols of Ur into an easier system. I only did as they did, for the symbols of my childhood were made with a stylus in clay from right to left. There was no smearing of indentions in a tablet, so it wasn't a problem. Let's see, perhaps you can hold the reed like so ~ Abram held his hand below the line he was writing ~ and not smear what you have written."
The boy's face brightened. "Let me try!, he said. "Hey! It works! Thank you, Father Abram, I will tell the others!"

A pang pierced Abram's heart at the inadvertent title given to him by the boy. He hid his pain and smiled, "Lesson's done for the day, Baruch! Practice the symbols and tomorrow I will show you how to form them into words that our friends know but our enemies do not." The young boy ran off to show his friends the new things his mentor had taught him.

As Abram put away the writing materials, a courier came running up with a message from Eliezer. It seemed that the herdsmen of Lot had been complaining that they were being slighted in the rotation of good grazing land. They had taken matters into their own hands and had forced their herds onto pasture that had been designated for Abram's oxen. Abram almost decided to overlook the matter except for one final notation by his chief under-shepherd which read, "Lot's men and your men almost came to blows over the fields. The Canaanites and Perizzites witnessed this, and were happy for it." Abram sighed, knowing that this day had been coming for several years. Since they had returned from the land of Egypt, God had blessed the herds and flocks of both Abram and Lot mightily and the land could no longer support both if they remained together. It was time to call a family meeting. Abram took back out the writing materials and slowly, but deliberately crafted a message for his nephew, Lot.

~~<Θ>~~

Lot made his way back to his tents at the end of another night shift with the flocks, the moon rising late in the night sky lighting his way. He was tired. A hill lion had taken a newborn lamb earlier in the dark of night. The shepherds could not find where the ewe had bedded to give birth until after the attack. The bleating of the mother had finally led them to the scene, but it was too late. The opportunistic predator had sensed what was happening and waited for the birth before attacking, seizing the newborn lamb and dragging it off to its doom, the afterbirth still attached. It must have been an old lion, for it left the mother alone. Tomorrow, they would have to hunt it down before it strikes again. Lot sighed. Some of the younger shepherds felt that the loss of a newborn was an ill omen, a sign that God was angry. He has seen it so much in his lifetime, he gave it not a second thought – it was just the way things were. All in all, the births were on the rise, and the flocks were healthy and growing. That created the real problem, not the loss of a lamb now and then, it was the fact that the hills of Bethel and Ai could no longer support the flocks. It took time for the grass to recover and they had to drift further and further south which spread their flocks and shepherds thinner and thinner.   As he pushed open the flap to his tent, he spied the parchment with Abram's distinctive writing laying on his pallet in the moonlight.   Ziphah was not in the tent, probably bedding down with the girls since Lot was scheduled to work all night. Lot took an unlit lamp out and carried the message out near the fire and lit the lamp to read the message. Abram wanted to meet under the trees on the hill overlooking the plains for lunch. He did not say what he wanted, but Lot knew in his heart what was coming. He snuffed the wick out with a quick snap of his licked fingers, and then turned back to the tent to get a few hours of sleep before the meeting with his uncle at noon.

"The land can no longer support us, my brother. Let us not argue over the best grazing. I will take the hill country and you can take the plains, or I will take the plains and you can take the hill country – I will leave the choice to you.", said Abram to Lot, as they finished up their meal together. He indicated with his right and left hands the two choices.

Lot was silent for a few moments, then spoke, "I will take the plains to the south and east – down toward Sodom and Gommorah. The waters of the Jordan spread out and water the land there well, just as the Nile does for the Delta area we briefly lived in. The cities close by will be a good place to trade and will offer Ziphah a distraction that she craves from the tent life. I will travel south."

"Only one warning, my nephew, do not hearken to your wife too much in this, she would have you become a city dweller again. I hear stories of the southern cities that remind me much of what we left in Ur. There is no fear of the One True God in those lands. Take heed to honor God and avoid sin.", said Abram.

"The old mischievous Lot cracked a smile, "Why do you always call me 'nephew' when you are talking to me thusly, but 'brother' when we are talking trades?" "Honestly, sometimes I think you think you are Terah, our father."

Abram tried vainly to suppress a smile, "He's not here with us to keep you in line, so someone has to do it....er, I mean at least try to do it."

The two men embraced and slapped each other on the back, knowing that their journeys together were at an end. As they turned to go, Abram had one final word to say, "I love you, Lot. And I will do whatever I have to, to see you succeed. If you ever need me, just say the word. We, the sons of Shem, must stick together against all others."

Lot's eyes briefly reddened, but he shook it off. "And I will do whatever I can for you, as well."

After the departure of Lot and his family, flocks, herds, and servants, Abram waited on God for instruction. One day, not long after Lot's exodus to the south, as he rested inside his tent at Bethel, the Lord spoke to him:

Abram! Abram! Lift up your eyes to the north, and to the south, and to the east, and to the west! All the land you see is yours and your descendants' forever! I will make your children as the dust of the earth, they will be without number, so vast will your descendents be. Arise, walk up and down this land, for I give it to you and to your descendents forever.

He broke camp and traveled as God had instructed him throughout the land of Canaan. He then settled in Hebron as his base of operations and built another altar there to the Lord God. His favorite encampment grew to be by the terebinth trees of Mamre, a friend and ally. There he continued to trust the Lord God concerning His promises. Sarai was encouraged by the words of God to her husband and seemed to snap out of her depressed state of mind. Once more, her laughter filled the air for Abram; and although she missed Ziphah and the twins, for she had counted them almost as her own, Sarai kept busy at the loom working with both wool and occasionally some cotton that came their way through the traders that roamed the land. All in all, living in Canaan was working out fine.

Chapter 13

War and Rescue

Chedorlaomer was in a fit of rage. The envoys from Bera, vassal king of Sodom, and from Birsha, vassal king of Gomorrah, were long overdue. These were at the southern reach of his empire which stretched from the Zagros mountains, across the Arabian desert, and down the eastern side of the Jordan river all the way to the Red Sea. They thought they could escape paying the tribute due to the Elamite Empire. From his palace in Susa, his spies were telling him that a conspiracy had arisen between the two, and that they had dragged in three of the smaller cities, such as Admah, Zeboim, and Bela with promises of independence. This rebellion had to be stopped or it would spread! For twelve good years the subdued Canaanite areas had regularly paid their tribute to keep the peace, but now they thought they were strong enough to keep Chedorlaomer from his due. He would have to plan this campaign carefully, using his allies from all over Mesopotamia. Let them think they have achieved their goals, it will take at least a year to muster and march an army south, destroying everything along the way. They will hear of the conquest of Bashan long before they see his troops, and they will rue the day they thought they could escape him.

Bera sent his own personal cupbearer to Birsha with the news that Chedorlaomer had amassed an army and was traveling south conquering everything in his path. He had already defeated the Rephalim tribes of Bashan and was marching on Mount Seir. They had little time to head off the invasion that was coming their way. Bisha called for a council of the kings to meet in Sodom. The met in the chambers of the palace in an improvised war room with a table in the center.

"Is there no other way but war?", asked Shinab, king of Admah, a town of the southeast Salt Sea region.

Bera rolled his eyes. "There will be no appeasing Chedorlaomer with gifts or tribute now, my dear Shinab, he is out for blood."

Shemeber, king of Zeboiim, remarked, "We discussed all this thoroughly last year when we decided to stop sending the annual tribute money to Susa. It was a calculated risk, we knew he might come, but we did not think he would.

"What are our options?, asked the king of Bela.

Birsha rolled out a lambskin scroll with a map of the area inked on it and proceeded to theorize the projected approach of the armies of Chedorlaomer from the north, "He will have to pass through the valley of Siddim. It is a place where we can divide his troops and make short work of them. The tar pits will nullify his cavalry and chariots. Our scouts estimate that they have no more than 4,000 troops and 50 charioteers, with 100 on mounted horseback for this campaign. We should be able to raise an equal amount of foot soldiers to his, and unless he has something hidden we do not know about, we should be able to repel his forces."

Bera nodded in agreement. "Once he gets a taste of Canaan's might, he will retreat back to Elam and not bother us again."

Shinab looked nervous as he asked his next question, "Are you sure we can defeat him? The Rephaim are giants! They are mighty men of great strength and size, and yet his forces defeated them easily. I hear that he has Amraphel, the son of Nimrod, as one of his generals."

Bera cut him off with a slap of his palm on the table, "Slink back to Admah if you want! We can defeat him without your paltry few soldiers, if you are so afraid of Chedolaomer! Why did you agree to join this uprising anyway if you were going to be negative about the whole affair?"

"Now, now, Bera; let's give him some leeway here", said Birsha, "his question is a legitimate one.   As tactical advisor in the military campaign let me tell you this, it won't be easy, but if we choose the battle site, we should win. By reports filtering in, Amraphel is indeed a part of the confederacy of kings that Chedorlaomer has put together with the promise of spoils and riches, but he is not his father. He has not successfully waged a campaign on his own. The other kings are Arioch and Tidal, both bringing only 1,000 troops each to the battle. The main influx of troops are from Chedorlaomer himself.   Amraphel commands the calvary and chariots, which will be useless in the Vale of Siddim. Once we get their forces turned, we will be able to pursue them north and take everything they brought and won from the Rephaim. Shinab, the Rephaim are big, yes; but they are slow and clumsy and make poor soldiers, that is why they were defeated so easily." "The Amorites and Amalekites were caught unprepared and could not bring but a small force against the invaders." He rolled the map back up and said with satisfaction, "I'm confident of victory and quite pleased with how things are turning out, we should come out better than if he had not invaded the south at all."

Chedorlaomer consulted with his fellow kings as they made their approach from the north toward the Pentapolis of the Jordan plains. He studied the faces of his generals to see which of them he would trust with his secret force of archers, trained by an old Egyptian soldier who had settled in the north. They had not yet seen battle in the easy victories against the Rephaim tribes of Bashan and the small forces of the Amorites and Amalekites. He was holding them back for now. He decided that quick deployment was of the essence and so he selected Amraphel as the one to deploy his archers to the flank of the enemy. His scouts had warned him of the asphalt and tar pits of Siddim and he was not going to fall for his opponents' ploy to have his men get bogged down in the treacherous terrain.

"Amraphel, how many horses will you have, if you leave the chariots sitting in camp?", asked Chedorlaomer.

"Amraphel looked started at the thought, "Why, each chariot uses two horses, so we would have between 200 and 250 horses available for mounts, with the reserve horses."

"Excellent! I want you to command my trained archers, which have been kept back until now, in the coming battle. We will not charge the enemy directly with our foot soldiers, at first. Instead, give each archer a horse and, at my signal, direct them to both flanks of the enemy where they will dismount and fire at will at their troops. The trap they set for us with the tar pits of Siddim will prove to be their own undoing, for they will not be able to hold formation under crossfire. For good measure, let every archer fire two arrows dipped in lit oil into the tar pits and see if they ignite. Let us see if we can rout the enemy quickly and end this rebellion.", said Chedorlaomer.

A slow grin came upon the face of Amraphel as he realized the tactical superiority that was being suggested. The other two kings nodded in agreement, knowing that Chedorlaomer's plan was brilliant. They should lose much fewer troops this way and gain more spoil.

The sun rose over the eastern horizon, spilling its rays into the shallow valley of Siddim. The black bubbling pools of tar belched noxious gases into the air, making the eyes water in the waiting troops of the Kings of the five cities of the Plain. Some who stood too close to the pits were losing their breakfast, as well. The troops were in close formation, awaiting the arrival of the forces of Chedorlaomer. While Birsha, king of Gommorah, seemed almost giddy with anticipation; Bera, king of Sodom, was more subdued.

"Something's not right, Birsha.", Bera said, "They should be at the north end of the vale by now."

"Keep your sandals tied", said Birsha, "they'll be here. They are likely still feeling the effects of their victory drinking last night."

"I'm not so sure, Birsa, I am going to take my honor guard and scout to the east to see if they are flanking the valley.", said Bera. "If we catch sight of them, our trumpeter will signal with one long blast."

"All right, if it will set your mind at ease, go on.", said Bishra, "you're going to miss the main battle, however."

"Humor me.", said Bera, "I will be back soon if there are no troops to the east. The brightness of the rising son could hide them from us, unless we look for them."

Bera rode off with a small contingency of his personal guard. Birsha watched him go with satisfaction. "I'll get all the glory for this great victory now.", he thought to himself.

In just a few minutes, Birsha heard the long drawn out blast of a shofar from the east. He muttered, "Well, it seems that Bera was correct, they were trying to flank us!" He issued the command for the troops to face the east to await the charge of the enemy, squinting in the face of the sun. He heard a faint sound like a light wind moving in the trees, when suddenly the air was filled with raining arrows from both the east and the west. In a matter of moments, almost half of his troops were dead or dying. Then he saw a flaming arrow arc toward one of the tar pits. The pit was belching gas as the arrow arrived and suddenly flaming hot tar was also raining onto the troops nearby. It was too much, his troops were running in confusion, trying to escape the rain of arrows, flaming tar, and fear that filled the air. As Birsha turned to flee the Valley, an arrow suddenly blossomed from his own chest, like a wooden flower watered in blood. His last thought before he lost consciousness was, "How did this happen?"

Bera, king of Sodom, surrendered to the forces of Chedorlaomer and awaited his fate. The other kings were not so fortunate, having all perished in the brief battle of the Vale of Siddim. Chedorlaomer rode up to see a humbled survivor in Bera and realized that he was the sole surviving rebel king. He could not help but gloat. "So, you thought to rebel against the might of Elam? What do you think of your chances now?"

Bera fell prostrate before Chedorlaomer and the other kings of the north that came riding up. "Oh, mighty Chedorlaomer, king of kings, I surrender all of my kingdom to you and your might! I beg only that you spare my life and I will serve you in this place, knowing that you cannot be defeated and that when cities rebel, you are quick to punish and willing to travel far and wide to secure your reign".

An amused Chedorlaomer replied, "Rise! Bera, king of Sodom, count yourself fortunate that you live and none of your confederates do, for then I would be forced to choose one of you to govern this land for me while I killed the others. You survived, and so you are my choice. Now, after a short stay here in the south, I will return to Elam, conquering cities as I go. Do not forget, my dear Bera, who rules this land."

Bera rose, "Oh my King, I will not forget! To show my loyalty, let me tell you of the resources in my lands that are now yours. There is a nomadic Shemite chieftain named Lot who has vast flocks of sheep, goats, cattle, and asses. Take what you will of his goods and servants to help you in your campaign. He is very wealthy and comes from a lineage of wealth, as well."

"Lot did you say?", interjected Arioch, king of Ellasar. "He would not be a native of Ur, would he? It is an uncommon name."

"O Lord, I do not know, his wife Ziphah, whom I know well, is from Harran and lives in Sodom, but his speech does sound more from Chaldea than hers."

"It must be! This same Lot left Ur many years ago after angering the priests of Nanna, Goddess of the Moon. I am a follower of her and her consort Sin and have heard the stories of how Lot and his brother Abram defiled the temple of Nanna and then fled, reportedly to Harran.", said Arioch.

"I know nothing of what you say, only that he is wealthy, having much livestock, herdsmen, and servants. He is learned in economics and attributes this to his father who is a trade caravan master of Harran. He would make a fine hostage, as I am sure that the ransom for him would be great.", said Bera.

"If he is, indeed, the same one who defiled the temple in Ur, then it would have to be a great ransom indeed to outdo the reward posted by the Chief Priest of Nanna for his return to Ur, for it is substantial.   Brother Kings! I say we apprehend this fugitive and take him back north with us.", proposed Arioch.

Chedorlaomer nodded, "Either way, it is to our advantage. We seize Lot, his people, his flocks and herds and we take them with us as we return home. We can determine later which would be more.... profitable; to ransom him to his father or to return him to Ur for the reward."

Abram had heard reports from his outlying herdsmen to the east and later the south of a mighty force that had made its way down the east bank of the Jordan and forded at Beth-barah to attack the forces of the Amalekites at Kadesh Barnea and the Amorites at Hazezon Tamar. Abram put his trained forces on alert for any signs of them turning back toward Hebron, where he headquartered his tribe under the terebinth trees of Mamre, an Amorite. He had made friends with three Amorite brothers through trading and the digging of wells that were beneficial to both parties, so he was alarmed when news came to him of the defeat of their kinsmen at the hands of the northern invaders. He was also concerned for his kinsman, Lot, for he was directly in the path of the forces if they turned back to the east and north toward the Pentapolis area of the Jordan plain.

He bowed low to God in prayer, "O most High God, there are none beside you, You alone are the God of Heaven and Earth! I pray Thee, protect my kinsman Lot from the hands of evil men. Keep the sword from his neck along with all he has. Give me guidance and strength to do what I must, if these men attack either him or me. Selah!"

He had no sooner finished his prayer when the three brothers, Mamre, Eshcol, and Aner arrived with a fourth man who was slightly wounded. Abram hurried to greet them and offer them food and drink, as befitting guests. Sarai and Hagar prepared the meal while the men talked.

"Abram, we have grave news concerning the forces from the north. They are four kings of Mesopotamia; Chedorlaomer of Elam, Amraphel of Shinar, Arioch of Ellasar, and Tidal of Goyim – they have brought forth an army of conquest to take of our lands. They have already conquered three tribes of the Rephaim of Bashan, the Amalekites in Kadesh, our kinsmen in Hazezon Tamar, and now this man tells us that they have routed the forces of the kings of the Pentapolis in the Valley of Siddim. Fortunately, their route took them away from us and they went around the Salt Sea and took spoils of the five cities. Their plan is to go north back home, conquering as they go. And Abram, they have taken your nephew Lot and all he has captive…", said Eschol, who was spokesman for the group.

Abram stood abruptly and gave quick orders to the leaders of his trained men to get themselves ready to depart, as the Amorite brothers listened with amazement.

"Did you not hear us, Abram? These men have already defeated everyone in their path – their forces outnumber us ten to one! We cannot hope to defeat them.", said Eschol.

Abram replied, "My God is with me. He will not leave me nor forsake me. He is mighty in battle and He will not let me fail. He made me a promise that my faith would be a blessing to all men. I find this challenge to be a test of that faith and I will not disappoint the One True God by sitting in my tents while my brother Lot languishes in bonds. I will free him from these men. I am from the area these men come from and I know their ways. I, with the help of my God, can defeat them. Will you go with me? If you will, I will reward you with the spoils of victory, and you can avenge your kinsmen."

The three looked at each other and nodded in assent, strengthened by the force of Abram's resolve. Sarai set lamb and goat's milk before the men and Abram lifted up his eyes to the heavens once again, "O Lord God, bless this food and drink, I pray, and bless our efforts to recover Lot and avenge our kinsmen against these idolaters who do not know you. Stretch forth Your mighty hand and strike down our foes that You may be known as the One True God in all the land. Selah!" With that, he sat down and began to eat while discussing battle tactics with the bewildered brothers who had known him beforehand only as a simple shepherd and digger of wells.

Chapter 14

"How many do we have again, Abram?", said an anxious Mamre to his friend.

"I have 318 trained men who are skilled in arms. They also each have a sword, a dagger forged from copper, and slings with a balanced pouch of stones. They are divided up into four troupes and are trained to coordinate their attacks through a series of trumpet blasts on a ram's horn. These men are tough, strong, and filled with courage – they will not retreat unless I issue the command. We will attack in the dark, that way the enemy cannot see our true numbers and gain heart. Our victory lies in surprise and confusion. If they do not know how few we are, then we can divide and rout them. We will wait until they are asleep to attack, that will only create more confusion.", said Abram.

"Where did you learn these things, Abram?", said Mamre, "You have never seemed to us to be more than a shepherd of flocks and a teacher of children. You now demonstrate the mind of a leader of soldiers."

"My father was a man who had his sons learn everything about his caravan business. I spent many years with the guards and soldiers who accompanied our caravans and was taught numerous lessons concerning military tactics and strategy. Did you know that to attack from the east is preferred in the morning and from the west in the evening?" ~ Mamre shook his head from side to side ~ "I thought not… it is to place the sun in the eyes of your enemy. But that, too, can be overcome if you put carved wooden covers with slits over your eyes and polish bronze shields to a shine to reflect the light back at your enemy. These are but a few things that commanders of men talk about around the campfires. Know this, Mamre, God expects us to use our minds – but I still trust Him to give us the victory. Many battles are lost over just one thing going wrong. If we lose the element of surprise…. say one of my trained men sneezes at the wrong time, then we can be the ones defeated. But I am confident that God will keep that from happening. We will win.", explained an assured Abram.

Mamre marveled at the faith of Abram in his God. He also found himself just a little envious of Abram's self-assurance. He had come along because his brothers had agreed to it and he was not a quitter, but he longed to return to Hebron and safety, for their small group was quickly gaining ground on the larger, slower force moving north. They were alongside the western bank of the sea of Kinneret, near to Laish and would probably overtake them that day. In fact, as he thought on these things, he heard Abram issue orders that the attack would take place that very night.

"I will take half our forces from the western flank of the encampment, Eliezer will take command of the rest of our men coming up from the south, the east is flanked by the waters of the great lake – we must give them a retreat, or else they will make a determined stand and overwhelm us. Their escape shall be to the north. We will pursue them through the night picking off stragglers as we go. The three Amorite brothers will be in charge of finding and securing the prisoners, who are our kinsmen and theirs.", detailed Abram, while drawing a crude map in the dirt with his staff. "Are there any questions?"

"Do we take prisoners or slay all?", asked one of the men.

"Neither, we will slay those we must and let the others escape – except for the kings. We must cut the head off the snake or it will return to strike us. Chedorlaomer, above all, must not escape. If spared, he will return with larger forces and ravage all of Canaan.", replied Abram. "Remember, wait in hiding a hundred paces from the edge of their camp, when you hear two short trumpets, charge the camp with as much noise as you can make – the confusion should cause then to be all turned around and not know who the enemy is until it is too late."

Two hours later, when Abram determined that all of his men were properly positioned, he gave the signal. His men rushed the sleeping camp, throwing it into utter confusion. As Abram had expected, the enemy forces were half drunk with wine. They were slow to respond, and his men quickly took out the ranking commanders of their opponents' armies. Abram moved swiftly through the camp, searching for the kings' tents. He and his men arrived just as Chedorlaomer emerged from a tent and mounted a horse to flee. Picking up a javelin from beside the prone body of a fallen enemy, Abram made a desperate throw at the retreating figure, but missed. As he gave orders to pursue, he received a message that Lot and his family had been found alive and well. Abram tucked his robe into his belt and took off after Chedorlaomer. His desperate throw with the javelin had not hit the fleeing king, but did hobble his horse in the rear right leg. After hours of pursuit and long past sunrise, Abram and his guards caught up with him. Although he was a great tactician, Chedorlaomer was no great personal warrior himself. He fell beneath a flurry of slung stones by Abram's men and died. Abram released his men to follow and spoil as many of the enemy as they wished and some went as far as Hobah, north of Damascus. Abram, however, returned to where Lot and the others were secured by the Great lake of Kinneseret.

Abram embraced Lot and said, "Once again, my nephew, I have had to get you out of a mess. I must confess, however, that this one was not of your own making, for once."

Lot replied, "Oh, I don't know... one makes enemies sometimes unawares. I heard talk of returning me to Ur to face the priests of Nanna for some sort of defilement of their temple some years back. Do you know what they might mean?", said Lot with a slight grin.

Abram rubbed his chin thoughtfully. "Let's see, Ur..... Ur? It seems I have heard of the place, although I can't for the life of me think of what you might have been doing in a temple.... I couldn't even get you to sacrifice to the One True God very often." Abram burst out laughing, and then took a more serious tone. "It seems that Dumazid, chief priest of Nanna, has a longer reach and memory than I would have thought....", said Abram, "I had almost forgotten about him."

The trip back south took them through the valley of Shaveh, a slight depression between two small hills outside of the Jubusite city of Salem, near the mountains of Moriah. As they passed by, men rode out of the city to greet them. As it turned out, news of Abram's great victory had gone before him and this was two kings and their honor guard coming to meet him.

"Blessed be Abram of the Most High God, possessor of heaven and earth: And blessed be the Most High God, which hath delivered your enemies into your hand.", said Mechizedek, priest and king of Salem, as he gave bread and wine to Abram.

Startled by the unexpected announcement, Abram took the proffered meal and gave it to his men. He then looked intently at the two contrasting kings and prayed silently for wisdom from God. The king of Salem was also a follower of the One True God – he could sense it, as well as, hear it in his words. He had heard rumors that Melchizedek was a man of mystery, no one knew his lineage or his origin. He took on faith that he was a righteous man and gave him a tenth of the spoils of war. He then turned to Bera, king of Salem, who was looking greedily at the people Lot had rescued.

"Congratulations on a great victory, Lord Abram! It seems you have done what I and the other kings of Canaan could not – rid us of Cheorlaomer and the Elamite Empire. We are in your debt.", Bera said.

"I sought only to rescue my kinsman and the remnants of my allies' kinsmen, as well.", said Abram humbly. "I offer you back your goods and spoils so that you may rebuild your city."

"No, Abram, the spoils and goods are yours by right of conquest – you take the goods, only give to me the people. I can use them as slaves to help rebuild the devastated cities of the plains.", said Bera.

"I will not enrich myself at your expense, King Bera, I seek only to allow my allies to take their rightful part and then the rest is yours - I will not take a thread or sandal of it – except what my men have eaten, I have sworn an oath to the Most High God. The people are to be freed. Lot, his family, and the people captured by the northern kings can return to their homes."

The evil king of Sodom, seeing his plan to enslave the captives evaporate, then reluctantly said, "As you wish, it is your right as champion of the battle. Go in Peace."

"Thank you, O King Bera. And may I also thank you, King Melchizedek, for your provisions and blessing of the Most High God.", said Abram.

Abram and Lot embraced once more, and then departed each to his own way; Abram, returning to the tents of Hebron, and Lot, returning with his wife and daughters back to Sodom. Abram pondered on the evil reputation of the king of Sodom and wondered if he would ever see his nephew again.

Chapter 15

Covenants and Complications

Years passed without incident as Abram busied himself with being the leader of his people. Sarai cried more often these days, as the change that affects all women had come upon her and she had given up all hope of producing an heir for Abram, a secret she kept from him. Abram sacrificed to the One True God and prayed to him often, thanking him for His bounty and provision. But He, like Sarai, had a child shaped vacuum in his life and wondered at the unfulfilled promise of an heir.

Then he had a new and different encounter with the One True God. This time it was not in a dream or a voice speaking in his mind. Abram was reclined in his tent one evening praying, for Sarai had already gone to sleep. Suddenly, a pinpoint of light grew in size in front of him. This time he *saw* the Lord God of Heaven and Earth. At least he saw the outline of Him, for He was so bright and shining that no man could see His face. It was if Abram looked at the outline of a man standing in front of the sun, only the brightness was emanating from the being instead of behind it. Abram fell down on his knees before Him and bowed low to the ground, quaking in fear.

"Do not be afraid, Abram. I am your shield, your exceedingly great reward."

Abram thought on everything he had been told by God before he stood to his feet. He was much troubled by the fact that Sarai had been unable to conceive a child. He had been clinging to the promises of God, but he could not but wonder about the delay. He was getting no younger. Meekly he asked the question he had pondered so often, "Lord, what about a child? Eliezar of Damascus is considered by tribal law to be my heir. Will you not give to me an heir? His children born in my tents will inherit all I have!"

This is not what will happen, instead, one born from your loins will be your heir.

Suddenly, without warning, Abram was no longer in his tent. He was standing on a knoll nearby overlooking some of his own sheep. He could see his herders nearby keeping watch over the flock by night. They did not seem to see him or his Heavenly visitor.

"Look up at the heavens, Abram, can you count the stars? So shall your descendents be without number. I am the Lord God who brought you out of Ur of the Chaldeans, to give you this land for an inheritance."

Abram, emboldened by these words, then said, "Lord God, how will I know this will happen? What would you have me do?"

"Bring me a three year old heifer, a three year old she goat, a three year old ram, a turtledove, and a pigeon to seal our covenant."

Abram spent the next several hours preparing for the coming ceremony. It took him until early afternoon to trap the birds requested. He brought them back to the bluff where God had showed him the stars. There he took the animals and cut them into two pieces and laid them apart from each other, with a path in between. The birds he placed one on the left and one on the right. Vultures began circling the carcasses and Abram had to use his staff to drive them away until late afternoon when they finally gave up and went away. Abram sat down, exhausted. Suddenly, he fell into a deep sleep as the sun was going down. He still heard the voice of the Lord speaking to him, even in his sleep.

"Know for a certainty that your descendents will sojourn in a land that is not theirs for four hundred years. After this time of affliction, the rulers of that land will be judged by me, and they will come out of that land with great possessions. As for you, you shall live to an old life in peace. But the fourth generation from the onset of captivity shall return to this land to make an ending to the Amorites for their sin."

Abram awoke in the dark. He saw a burning torch and a smoking firepot pass through the path between the cut pieces of the animals. God was pledging Himself to fulfill his words or He would become as the animals He passed between. He did not require Abram to do anything. He then spoke once more to Abram.

"I will give the land from the Nile River to the Euphrates River to your descendents in this covenant. The lands of the Kenites, the Kenezzites, the Kadmonites, the Hittites, the Perizzites, the Raphaim, the Amorites, the Canaanites, the Girgashites, and the Jubusites will belong to your descendents."

Abram bowed down and worshipped the Lord God of Heaven and Earth who condescended to make such a covenant with a mere man.

~~<Θ>~~

"His promise is to you, my husband, not to me.", said Sarai bitterly.

"How can you say such a thing? We are one flesh, you and I. Husband and wife! A promise to me is also a promise to you! God *showed* Himself to me, woman! This was no mere voice in my head this time! He took me from our tent Himself into the night and showed me the stars of the sky and said our descendents will be without number!", exclaimed Abram to his wife, who was slowly shaking her head side to side.

"Your descendents, Abram… Your covenant, Abram… Your heir of promise, Abram… not mine. I am too old to have children anymore. I cannot conceive – I am finished with that part of life. It is impossible for me, husband. The way of women is no longer mine, it hasn't been for quite some time now. I will never bear you a child.", said Sarai, tears streaming down her face as she saw each of her final words strike her husband like a dagger to his heart.

The color drained from Abram's face as he contemplated the impact of her words. He knew from his more than 75 years of experience with cattle, sheep, goats, and camels that the time came when the females could no longer give birth. He had never considered that Sarai could not have a child. He just knew it was going to happen when God was ready for it to happen. Now, he was faced with …. what? He was at a loss of understanding and was perplexed by her disclosure.

Sarai continued, "There is a way, however, for you to bear me a son. Take my handmaiden Hagar to your bed and she shall conceive us a child. It is my right to give her to you. She shall bear your son and heir, for us to raise together."

Abram reeled with the implications of what she was saying. "Sarai, you can't be serious! I have never been with another woman besides you! You are my life, my love, my all! I cannot take another woman in my arms and treat her as I do you! God made Eve for Adam and He made you for me. That is all there is to the matter… I won't do it."

"Then you shall never have a son. We will never have a son. It is the only way it can happen, husband. I have already talked to Hagar about this and she is willing to submit to my will in this matter. You are the only one standing in the way.", said Sarai decisively.

"You've already talked to her about this!? Before talking to me? Wife, I can't believe this! I tell you that God has promised us descendents without number and you tell me that I must sleep with Hagar to fulfill the promise? No, I cannot do this…. I must pray… and ask God for direction, for clarity, for an answer to this…problem."

"Abram, I tell you this because I love you and because I know that you must have a son. I cannot conceive the heir we need, but I can consent to you having an heir with Hagar, in my stead. Don't you see? It is as if the child were also mine this way, as much as any child can be mine.", she said. "We women keep track of these things and the time is right for her to conceive now, this very day. Go to her tent this very night, for she awaits you. You will only have to do this once if we do it right. The timing of this vision could not be more perfect for this. God will bless this brief union with a child – I know it!", said Sarai pleadingly.

"Woman, I cannot… not without praying first. Not without sacrificing to God, not without His instruction.", said Abram, shaking his head.

"Fine! Then go! Do your sacrifice, make your prayers, and wait another month for the right day – or two, or twenty, or forty-five years as I have waited for God to bless my barren loins!", said Sarai angrily, throwing his cloak at him. "Go!"

Abram left the tent in a daze, not believing what had just transpired. He made to go to the herds to pick out a goat for the sacrifice when his eyes fell upon Hagar's tent. He stood for long moment and stared, thinking of first, the tears; and then, the anger of his wife. Almost without realizing it, he was stumbling towards the beckoning tent, loosening his robes as he went.

~~<Θ>~~

"I am with child, mistress.", said Hagar to Sarai.

Sarai clapped her hands with joy and said, "I must be quick and tell Abram the wonderful news that we have a child on the way. Of course, we can't be sure it is a boy yet – but he will still be excited at the prospect of any child, at this point. If it is not a boy, we will have to try again, won't we?"

"With all due respect, mistress, shouldn't I be the one to tell him the news? After all, I am the mother.", said Hagar.

Sarai looked at Hagar in disbelief. "What do you mean by such a statement, this child is conceived because I allowed it – no, I *encouraged* it. It was my plan so that Abram and I could raise him a son."

Hagar refused to back down and looked Sarai in the eye, "This is my child, mistress, not yours. I conceived it and I will bear it and I will keep it. I don't know what you might have thought, but I will not give up my child to you."

Sarai could not believe her ears. Hagar had never acted this way. Since coming to live with them, she had been the model of compliance and gratefulness. But now, at this most important time in the life of Abram and Sarai, she was being obstinate and selfish and did not want to give up the baby. Sarai had no choice – she would have to discipline her for this dishonor, but first she must talk to Abram. She fled the tent in search of Abram, finding him near the teaching tent where he taught the children how to read and write.

"Husband, I must talk to you at once!", said Sarai.

"Abram heard the alarm in his wife's voice and questioned, "What's wrong, my princess?"

"It's Hagar. She has conceived your child – it was I who gave her into your embrace - and yet she refuses to honor our agreement to give up the child when it is born. She insists that she is the mother and will not allow it to be *our* child."

Abram's hands shook at the news that he had a child coming into the world, but was tempered by the facts of the situation that now presented itself. He knew that Sarai would never accept the unborn child on Hagar's terms, so he thought to buy some time to think about the situation. "She is your handmaiden to do with as you see fit. It is your agreement with her, not mine. I will leave her in your hands.", he said.

Sarai, unsatisfied by this response, whirled and left Abram and found Hagar at her work. "My husband said for me to deal with you as I see fit. I want you to know that you have betrayed my trust and I will never allow my husband near you again. If this child is a boy, then he will live a miserable life in this camp. I will see to that. And if it is a girl, I will sell her to some passing caravan one day. This is how I deal with those who break their vows to me."

Hagar jutted out her jaw, "I made no vow to give up my child!"

Sarai retorted, "You made a vow to obey me, and you knew full well that when I sent my husband to your bed, it was for one reason – to bear a child for us, him and me!" She then took a cord of camel hair and hit Hagar across the face with it. "Betrayer!", she shouted.

Hagar ran, stumbling, from the tent in terror at the hatred in Sarai's voice. She determined to return to Egypt and have her child there. She gathered a few things from her tent and ran southward into the hills. Many days later, she found herself at a spring near the Egyptian border. She was planning her next move, for she knew not how to enter Egypt without the news eventually getting back to the royal family, who would send for her and probably imprison her or worse. While she was thinking on these things, a man arrived at the spring and knelt to drink.

Standing, he turned and addressed her by name, "Hagar, handmaiden of Sarai, why is it that you are here and where are you going?"

Startled, she blurted out, "I am fleeing from the face of my mistress, Sarai."

The man began to glow softly, "Return to your mistress and submit to her commands. Thus says the Lord God unto you,

"Behold, you are with child and will bear a son. You shall call his name Ishmael, for the Lord has heard your affliction. He shall be strong and untamed with many enemies, yet he shall live among his brethren. I will multiply your descendents exceedingly, they shall

be without number."

Hagar bowed her head before the angel of the Lord and spoke, "You are the God who sees me. I have been a servant for many years now in the tents of Abraham, I who once thought to be the consort of a Pharoah. And now, you have restored to me my hope of a heritage, a lineage, a name... I shall call this place Beer Lahai Roi, which means 'the well of Him who sees and gives life'." She left the Sinai and headed northwest toward Hebron and the tents of Abram pitched under the trees of Mamre, the Amorite.

Chapter 16

"I don't want her back. She left and deserted me and the camp and she does not deserve to come back, husband!", said an angry Sarai to Abram.

"But her story has the ring of truth to it, Princess, it sounds just like what God would do; make her come back to us, I mean. She says the child will be a boy! Let's wait and see if it is. The Lord even named the child, Sarai! Ishmael – 'The Lord sees our affliction' - what an appropriate name for a child born to us in our declining years.", defended Abram.

"Your child, not mine! She made that perfectly clear before she left. She plans to use this child to curry your favor and to displace me as your wife! I can see it now, the beautiful young Hagar, wife of Abram the Hebrew! You might as well throw me out with the bath water now!", shouted Sarai.

"Now, now, Sarai, don't talk like this. No one could ever replace you, my love. I only went to her bed once, at your insistence I might add. You are my Sarai, my princess, my love. This woman means nothing to me, I assure you. The child, on the other hand, means everything.... to me and to you. If it is a boy, we will know that the Lord has sent her back and the child shall be ours. The Lord also told her to do whatever it is that you tell her to do, to submit to you –so *if* you tell her to give up the child, she will have to do so. Isn't that right?", reasoned Abram.

Sarai calmed down at the words of Abram. "I will agree to her return on the condition that once the child is weaned, he stay no more in her tents but in ours!", said Sarai. "I want to raise this child, husband, as if it is my very own."

"As do I, my sweet, as do I."

The time passed swiftly and the child was born, a swarthy, dark baby boy full of life and energy. As ordered by the Lord, the name of the child was Ishmael. Hagar was a model servant to Sarai, understanding the will of the God who sees her. But in her heart of hearts, she grieved for the day that her boy would no longer nurse at her breast, for then, the child would be in the tents of Abram and Sarai until his marriage. He would be lost to her, unless she could devise a strategy to keep him. She thought long and hard about it, but nothing came to her. Abram was attentive to the child, as he was to all of the children, but Sarai was strangely aloof when Ishmael was around, almost as if she didn't know what to do about him.

One day, Sarai asked Hagar to bring Ishmael to her for her to hold. Although Hagar bristled at the prospect of Sarai holding her baby boy, she obeyed. Sarai looked at the high forehead typical of the Egyptians, and the dark bronze skin of the child and pushed him back at Hagar. "One would almost think you had gone to Egypt to get pregnant, Hagar – this child looks nothing like a Hebrew.", she retorted.

Hagar's eyes flashed in anger at the insensitive remark. She looked down quickly as her cheeks colored, "I assure you, his father is Lord Abram. I have never been with another man. Ever."

"Yes, yes, I trust that is true. Only, he is so… Egyptian. He makes me shudder to think what would have happened had I been used by Pharoah. He reminds me of that awful time when I thought I was going to be taken by a man not my husband.", said Sarai.

"Oh, I wouldn't know what that is like, my mistress.", said Hagar ironically, "Ishmael reminds me of home, of the Nile, of my life before…."

Sharply, Sarai studied Hagar's face to see if there be any deceit and found none.

Satisfied, she then said, "You may continue to keep Ishmael in your tents, Hagar, even past his weaning. He is a comfort to you and a dread reminder to me. I will speak to Abram about it."

Hagar's heart soared as she heard the words of Sarai. In her heart, she thanked The God Who Sees for doing what she could not – change the mind of Sarai.

The days passed into years uneventfully. The life of a nomadic herder of sheep, goats, cattle, asses, and even camels never fully becomes routine, as it is a constant search for good pasture for the flocks and herds. Then there are the times of the year when they shear the sheep and when they travel to market in the cities and sell off livestock; but for the most part, life is simple. Ishmael continued to grow into a young boy and then a young man. Sarai eyed the boy and his mother suspiciously, ever looking for the least bit of attention paid to the pair by Abram that might signify any feelings for Hagar. There were none. However, Abram made his feelings for Ishmael quite clear – he loved the boy immensely and took every effort to teach him all the ways of the camp. He taught him the symbols that were used by the Hebrews for writing messages and made sure that Ishmael could not only write them, but read and understand what was written. He allowed the boy to train with the men in the art of self-defense using the sword, the dagger, the staff, and the sling.

On the thirteenth anniversary of Ishmael's birth, Abram called the people together for a celebration. He sacrificed to the Lord God of Heaven and Earth and then had his servants prepare a feast for the multitude of men and their families that were gathered together with them at Hebron, under the trees of Mamre. It was a holiday to remember for Abram's tribe, the Hebrews.

At noontime on the final day of the feast, three men approached the tent of Abram from the east, dressed in white. Abram, alarmed by the sudden appearance of strangers, while all his people were together, stood up and swiftly approached the mysterious trio. As he approached, he heard the voice of the Lord speak to him in his heart:

Abram! I am El Shaddai, the Almighty God! Walk before me in innocence and my covenant with you shall be established. I will multiply your descendents exceedingly."

Abram ran up to the three strangers and bowed down low, trembling; for he knew that these were messengers of the Most High God.
"My Lord, if I have found favor in your sight, please come and visit with me. I will bring water to wash your feet and bread that you may be refreshed. Then you may continue on your journey.", said Abram humbly.

He called Sarai over and instructed her to make haste to prepare three bread cakes for the visitors out of their finest flour. He then hurried to find a choice young calf that he gave over to a servant to butcher and prepare for them. He took all that was prepared with goat's milk and curds in a pottery bowl for the three men and stood by as they reclined beneath the terebinth trees and ate.

"Where is Sarah, your wife, Abraham?", asked one of the visitors.

Abram was puzzled. He dare not question the use of different names than the ones he and Sarai had had for all their lives – so he said, "She is in the tent."

"I will return next year at this time and when I do – Sarah shall have a son.", announced the man.

Sarai, who was standing behind the man in the door of the tent overheard his comment and laughed a small bitter laugh, thinking to herself, "Doesn't this man know I am barren? I am old, ninety years have I lived on this earth and the way of women left me when I was seventy-five! Does he think I will find pleasure in his mockery of my lot in life?"

The man began to glow softly. *"Why did your wife laugh, Abraham? Does she think she is too old for this? Is there anything too hard for the Lord God? You will have a son at the appointed time next year!"*

Sarah came out of the tent to defend herself, "I did not laugh." She saw the man and became frightened, for she then knew he was no ordinary man.

"Yes you did, Sarah – this shall be your new name – for your son shall bring forth kings unto this earth. You will be the mother of many nations and you shall call your son Isaac, for you laughed when you were told by the Lord what He would do. I will establish my covenant with Isaac and not Ishmael forever." He turned to Abram and then said,

"Abraham shall be your new name, for no longer shall people call you Abram – for you will be called the father of many nations."

Abraham fell on his face before the Lord and laughed also and said, "Oh, that Ishmael might live before you too! How is it that man one hundred years old and a woman who is ninety years old can have a child?"

The Lord continued, *"Sarah shall bear you a son and Isaac shall have the everlasting covenant of God upon him and his descendents. I will also bless Ishmael, for your sake. He will be fruitful and he will multiply exceedingly and shall father twelve princes, and become a great nation also – but my covenant will I establish with Isaac, who will be born to Sarah at this season next year."*

Abraham was incredulous – The Lord God of Heaven and Earth had visited him, not in dreams and visions – but in person!

The Lord continued, *"This shall be the sign of our covenant together. Remember how I walked between the cut pieces of sacrifice without asking you to do so? Now, I require this of you and your descendents: every male to be circumcised in their foreskin on their eighth day. Your descendents and all your servants shall take this sign or be cut off from the covenant I established with you forever."*

Abraham arose from off his face and stared at his visitors. He looked over at Sarah and said, "Go, wife, and tell the others those things which the Lord has made known to us today. Make preparations for our obedience to the will of the Lord. Make it known that anyone who is not willing to take the sign of the covenant is free to leave, but they can never come back unless they are willing to submit to the One True God, who asks us to do this simple thing. We will obey the Lord today – from me to Ishmael to every goat herder of our tribe."

Sarah, trembling, turned to go. She looked over her shoulder in wonder at men and contemplated the sudden turn of events in her life. Hope sprang into her heart as she thought on the promise – A son, a son, A SON! She was beside herself with eager anticipation, giddy with the news, yet sobered by the task at hand. This was going to be a day to remember.

~~<Θ>~~

Abraham walked with his visitors, two of whom had not spoken a single word, to the bluff overlooking the valley which spread out to the east. In the far distance you could just see parts of the Jordan River as tributaries from it meandered through the fertile area east of the Salt Sea, where all water eventually drained. The towns of Canaan dotted the landscape - one could see the haze in the air that marked where the two largest settlements, Sodom and Gomorrah, were. Abraham looked out, longing after his nephew Lot, to tell him the good news concerning the promise of God. It had been years since they had seen one another. News had filtered back to Abraham that Lot had finally given in to Ziphah's wishes and moved into Sodom. After their close call at being kidnapped years earlier, Ziphah had steadfastly refused to move back into the tents. She was a city girl and she wanted her daughters raised there, as well. They would be getting on to young womanhood by now. Abraham had heard snatches of conversations from caravan people passing through about the way both of those cities had descended into debauchery after their liberation from the Elamite kingdom by Abraham's men. "Some people, when free, do not know how to handle freedom.", thought Abraham.

Suddenly, the spokesman for the group stopped walking, while the other two continued on toward the east and south. *"Shall I hide from Abraham what I am planning to do since he will become such a mighty nation, and in him will all the nations of the earth be blessed?"*, said the man, who once again began to glow softly as he spoke.

"The outcry against Sodom and Gomorrah is great and their sin is exceedingly grave. I will visit them and see for myself and know if it is so.", said the man.

Abraham stood before the heavenly messenger and asked, thinking of Lot, "Will you sweep away the righteous with the wicked? Suppose there are fifty righteous men in the city....will you not spare the wicked for the righteous' sake?"

"I will spare the city if I find fifty righteous men.", said the Lord.

"I am but dust from the earth, but I wonder…. If there were five lacking form the fifty, would you still spare it? Seeing you are a merciful God and Judge the earth with justice.", said Abraham.

"*I will spare the city for the sake of forty-five righteous men.*", said the Lord.

"Suppose forty are found there? What then?", Abram reasoned.

"*I will spare the city for the sake of the forty.*", said the Lord.

"Oh, do not be angry with me, Lord, as I plead for the righteous! What about thirty?"

"*I will spare the city for the sake of the thirty righteous.*"

"I have spoken and bargained with you, Lord, and will do so again – what about twenty?"

"*If I find twenty righteous in the city, I will spare it for the sake of the twenty.*"

Please do not be angry with me, this is my final appeal – suppose ten righteous are found – will you not spare them all?"

"*If ten righteous people are found in the city, I will spare the whole.*"

Abram watched the two messengers as they went behind a hill out of sight and suddenly realized that he was standing alone on the bluff. He turned and made his way back to the camp where the knives were being sharpened for the task ahead.

Chapter 17

Sodom and Gommorah

The two messengers grimly made their way toward the city of Sodom. On their way, far south of where they had left Abraham, they happened upon a small caravan making its way north toward Hebron. The caravan leader, a trader name Mahmullaq, got off his camel to engage them in conversation, plying his wares. He approached them with a broad grin on his face. Their heads were wrapped with a *soderah* of pure white, matching their robes. He wondered as he approached how they kept them so clean from the dust of the road.

"Ah, travelers! Interested in cloth from Egypt? Dried and pressed dates? No? How about a slave? I picked up some man-servants in Sodom and even a few young women in Gomorrah suitable for concubines...."

"We are not interested in purchasing flesh, trader, or anything else for that matter.", said one of the messengers.

At these words, Mahmullaq's countenance fell and he looked quickly back at his camel, sensing that there was no profit to be made here.

"However... we might be interested in another commodity, for which we will compensate you in accordance to its value."

The grin returned. "Ah, if it is not of a physical nature... then the most desired 'commodity' is usually....information.", said the caravan leader.

"I see we are speaking the same language now.", said the messenger. "My companion and I are looking for someone. He is the relative of a friend. His name is Lot."

"Ah, Lord Lot, the Hebrew – nephew, some say brother, of the great man Abram, who rescued this land from the clutches of Chadorlaomer years ago. Yes, I know him well – having dealt with him on many occasions. He is currently living – wait, before I tell you this – who is it that has sent you? I would not like to make an enemy of Lord Abram, who is blessed by the One True God and has many friends in Canaan because of his goodness."

"Abraham, as Abram is now called, is the relative we spoke about. We have a message to deliver to Lot. Our last report was that he was encamped near Sodom, but that was some time ago. As this message needs to be delivered without delay, we need his most current location. We will pay you for it."

"No need, no need – if you were looking for the most profitable trades to be made in the five cities, I would charge for that sort of information.... But this is just common courtesy. Let us say, a favor.... Lot is currently residing in the merchant ward of Sodom. His wife persuaded him to leave the tents to his herders. He conducts his business from his home there, but is frequently in the fields with his flocks, which are many. He is probably one of the richest men in

Sodom. His two daughters are considered the most eligible catches in town, and have remained in his home, unspoiled by the vices of that depraved city. Bera, the king of Sodom, has offered to take them into his harem, but Lot has so far refused his offer."

"So Lot can be found *in* Sodom, instead of outside of Sodom?", repeated the messenger.

"For the most part, except when he is monitoring his herdsmen and checking on the flocks", said the trader.

An errant wind blew down the part of the *soderah* that covered the face of one of the travelers, Mahmullaq was stunned to see chiseled features with no beard... and golden blond hair, a rarity in this land. They both had piercing blue eyes, also rare, but not unknown in the region. He spoke the next words in a lowered voice, "If you plan to travel to Sodom, you might be interested in something else I can sell you. I see no weapons on your person. You might want to have a sword, or at least a small dagger to protect yourself. The Sodomites are aggressive, and if they see your countenance, may wish to enslave you....or worse."

As he fastened back the cloth across his face, leaving only his eyes showing, the unnamed traveler spoke, "We have no need of weapons, I assure you. We are well capable of defending ourselves without them." He thought for a moment, looked upward, and then, almost as if making a decision, said, "I have valuable information I will share with you, Mahmullaq, since you have been so honest and forthcoming with us.", said the messenger, "Do not waver in your way north, trader, and do not ever plan on visiting the cities of the plains again. God is going to bring judgment on the wickedness of that land."

Mahmullaq blanched at the use of his name, for he had not given it. He perceived that these were no ordinary men and understood the truth of what they were saying. He thanked the men and wished them a good journey, for they were only a day's walk from the beginning of the cities of the plains, and then he quickly mounted his camel and gave the command for the caravan to move on – north, as fast as they could and as far as they could from the coming doom to the area.

~~<Θ>~~

It was a day like any other. The sun rose in the east, beautiful in splendor as it colored the horizon's clouds with streaks of red, pink, and amber against an azure sky. The herds of cattle along with flocks of sheep and goats dotted the landscape as the world woke up to a crisp, early spring morning. The Jordan River sparkled in the sunlight as it meandered through the valley of the plain, branching off into several unnamed tributaries which spread east and west before coalescing once more into the Salt Sea. Flowers were budding; bees were beginning to send out workers to scout for the coming harvest of pollen and nectar.

Near to one of the tributaries, a woman dipped her pot into the clear, cold rushing water to collect enough for the morning meal and to fill her husband's water skin for the long day ahead. Beside her, her small son made a crude boat from a piece of bush bark, and watched it sail in the swift current of the small river, running along its banks laughing until a bend took the boat out of sight. The woman called to her son, who turned and walked back to the path where she waited. He took one last look over his shoulder at the water, stooped to pick up a stone, turned and flung it into the deepest part of the water where it made a satisfying sound as it hit. The pool where the stone hit was calmer water than where he had sailed his boat and made ripples that spread out. The pair watched for a moment, hand in hand, and turned and made their way back to the encampment beyond the bluff to join their family for breakfast, the woman balancing her water pot on her head with one hand, and grasping the small hand of her son in the other. If they had stayed just a few more minutes before they left, they would have noticed the change that took place in the pool where her son threw his rock. At first, it was small. Just a few bubbles, then, almost as if someone had opened a gate, the water began to boil furiously, releasing pent up gas into the atmosphere. This was not just happening at this spot, however, it was happening in at least two dozen places spread far and wide across the plains, most notably, it was happening at the wells in all of the cities, except Bela, which had changed its name to Zoar after the loss of their king. A colorless, odorless, gas was rising from the depths of the earth. The atmospheric conditions were keeping the gas close to the ground, for there was no wind that day. Like a pot with a lid on it, the pressure began to build as the day moved on. And not one single solitary person noticed it. To them, it was a day like any other. Only it was not.

~~~<⊖>~~~

At noontime, the two messengers stopped at a well outside of Sodom to ask directions to the merchant ward, and the house of Lot. There were several men loafing around the well, not having found any daily work, most of them not wanting to. One of the men, a large sallow faced man with narrow eyes asked them where they were from. The spokesman for the two replied, "We come from north to deliver a message to Lord Lot from his kinsman."

"Lot, you say? I know him. We all do... he thinks he's better than the people of Sodom, living apart from us in the merchant ward so his daughters won't have to walk among us. Our king isn't even good enough for them! Why, you men have the look of being of the same attitude... you won't even show us your face! Take that wrapping down so we can get a good look at you.", said the man, whose name was Midsal. He approached the duo threateningly.

"The day has been warm and our journey dusty", said the messenger, who unfastened his *soderah* as he spoke calmly, "please, may we drink from the well? We meant no offense."

Taken aback by the calm response, Midsal did not know what to do next. He had expected resistance, and was prepared to physically enforce his demand. But now, he took the drawing gourd and lowered it into the water and drew out water which he turned and offered to the pair of strangers. The others watched on; puzzled, because it was a known fact that Midsal was a cruel bully who delighted in the misery of others. This was out of character for him. He looked into the clear blue eyes of the stranger and glimpsed the golden hair rimming his face and was startled. Almost in a trance, he lifted the gourd to the stranger's lips and watched him drink. He shook his head, almost as if coming out of a dream.

"My but you are a pretty man.", he said. "We don't see many people with your coloring in this part of the land. Where did you say you were from?"

"North... far north. We have traveled far to speak with Lot, so if we may, could you point us the way to the merchant ward, where we may complete our business in Sodom."

"Now, let's not be hasty, strangers, the people of Sodom might want to get to know you better before you go." He winked at one of his companions as he spoke. "Our king, Bera, has orders to bring all strangers to him for inspection before allowing them free access to our city. He is afraid of spies coming down from the north, from Elam, to be exact. You would not happen to be from Elam, would you?"

"No, we would not. But if that is the law, then we will gladly submit to it. Take us to see King Bera, then, we will finish our business with Lot."

Midsal motioned to two of his cronies to take position on either side of the strangers to insure that they did not make a break for freedom. He then led them to the gates of the city, where he took one of the guards aside and whispered to him, nodding in the direction of the two dressed in white. A small grin came to the face of the guard and he motioned them through. "A promise of reward from the king, if he is pleased.", muttered the brigand to one of his fellows. The guard has briefly thought about taking charge of the prisoners himself; but this way, he took no chances of displeasing his king by abandoning his post. Besides, Midsal had come through before; after all, he was married to a cousin, briefly, anyway.

They made their way through the marketplace, drawing stares from the people. The messenger had replaced his *soderah* so that only his eyes showed. Word traveled like wildfire in a town like Sodom. Rumors abounded as people speculated as to the nature and intent of the unusual pair. They were not like others who came and went on a regular basis, so naturally, people were curious and suspicious. Word came to the king by runner, as the group made their way across town to the palace. Bera, ever watchful, had his spies everywhere in town. Nothing happened in Sodom without he was told of it. So, as Midsal and his troupe made their way into the palace, the captain of the guard greeted him and said, "More 'strangers' for the king to approve, Midsal? My, you have been busy... this is the third such group this month." He said the word strangers almost with contempt, for he knew that Bera often imprisoned or enslaved anyone he remotely suspected of being in league with the cities of Mesopotamia. He had even had a few of them executed, when after torture, they confessed to being spies. It was tenuous thing, keeping trade with the cities of the north, but at the same time, staying independent of them. The captain escorted them into the king's chamber for his review.

The king, with his queen nearby, eyed the pair with a penetrating stare and made a motion to the guard who demanded that they remove their headgear. A sharp intake of breath followed from everyone in the room as the two men complied with the order and revealed themselves to be identical twins of extraordinary grace. Of common height, that was the only thing common about them. Their skin was bronze, almost a golden color with matching close cropped curly locks that framed classic features that were just too handsome to be true. The queen's mouth opened in amazement, for she had never seen such beauty in any man. The raw lust in her eyes was sudden and apparent and immediately noticed by the king. A man given to all sorts of evil passions, he too felt a sudden longing in his loins as he thought of these men stripped and naked before him. Bera thought to himself, "There will be time for that later, but first, I must find out why they are here." He leaned forward and said rapidly, "Welcome to Sodom, the flower of the plains! To what do we owe this unexpected pleasure? Where are you from and what business do you have in our fair city?"

The messenger responded, "We are travelers from the north, here to deliver a message to Lot from his kinsman, Abraham. We were told he resides in the merchant ward of this town."

Bera was disappointed and troubled by this response, for he knew that if they were connected to Abram, then he dare not touch them. As much as he wanted, he knew that he could not start a war with the man who had delivered the five cities from the power of the kings of the north. Abram was too well loved and had many allies in Canaan. His power over the cities of the plains would vanish at once if Abram desired it. One thing puzzled him, however, and he pressed for an answer. "You said 'Abraham', not 'Abram' sent you. Are we talking about the same person or is there another kinsman with a name so similar? I know Abram, but not Abraham."

"They are the one and the same person, the Lord God of Heaven having changed his name of late to reflect his new lineage as the father of many nations.", replied the messenger simply.

"Speaking of names, what is your name, traveler? And that of your brother?", asked the king.

"I am called Eshael and my fellow messenger is called Dunael."

Bera reacted as if struck. The names were fraught with meaning. Bera was a libertine, a coward, a pompous opportunist, but he was no fool. "Fire of God" and "Judgment of God"! Here in Sodom – a cold trickle of sweat ran down his spine to the small of his back as he contemplated his next move.

"Well, on your way to see Lot, you say? Guards, escort these two to the merchant quarter. See that they arrive safely at the home of Lot, the Hebrew. Oh, and men, allow them to cover their faces – we don't want a riot in the streets. Do greet Lord Lot for me and relay to him my best regards. Tell him my offer still stands. He and his family are welcome citizens of our city and hopefully, of my house."

The queen frowned with obvious disapproval as the two were led out and she hissed, "I wanted those men! I have never seen such beauty and we only saw their faces – I could not wait to see the rest of them and you let them go! Why?"

Bera turned to his wife and replied through thin, clenched lips, "Because I want to live to see another day, my dear. There is a power in those two that I fear. I may be king here in Sodom, but I have seen the combined might of four kings broken by the power of Abram's God. And, unless I am mistaken, these men were not just sent to see Lot by Abram, but also by his God. We had best leave these two alone, or else we will find our way of life will become a byword to the rest of the world."

She shook her head, not understanding a bit of what he was saying, she was so caught up in her own unbridled longing for the exotic twins. She could not get them out of her mind. She knew she must have them. She excused herself and sent secret orders for the pair to be brought back to her private chambers, as soon as they left Lot's house. She went to her chambers to prepare for a night of passion, for in her mind, no one could refuse the advances of a queen.

The messengers, Eshael and Dunael, were dutifully escorted directly to the home of Lot. Unfortunately, Lot was out in the fields and was not expected to return before nightfall. The pair decided, after a cool reception from Ziphah, to walk the streets of the city and get some firsthand experience with the people of Sodom, in hopes of finding the righteous. Their guards having departed back to the king's palace, the two set out on foot alone to the market in town, near the temple to Astoreth, the goddess of pleasure. It wasn't long before they ran into trouble. Men approached them and demanded that they disrobe. They refused. The men started to attack them when suddenly the two were just not there anymore. Confused, the men ran from street to street searching for the duo, convinced that they were tricksters who were hiding. The men came upon the guard and told them what had happened; and the guards, who had their own orders from the queen, spread out to look for the pair of travelers also. The whole city was in an uproar as the men had simply vanished into thin air. As the afternoon moved on, thick storm clouds gathered from the west and settled over the plains, building into the heavens until day began to look like night. Shop keepers gathered their goods and closed their booths, as people made their way home to weather the storm that was coming their way.

Midsal was unhappy. Not only had he not received a "finder's fee" for the pair of strangers he had brought to King Bera, he was now in debt to the guard at the city gate who now demanded his share of the bounty. He had built too good a case for the pair, it seems, sure that their depraved king would enslave the men and reward him handsomely. The guard did not believe him when he told him that Bera had turned them loose. He begged for a bit of time, and he was sure he could still turn a profit from the two, if he could only find them. He remembered that they were looking for Lot the Hebrew and so he set a watch on Lot's house and place of business to notify him as soon as they showed up. It wasn't long until a youth came running up to him with a message that the pair had left Lot's house and headed for the market. He gathered three of his friends, other ne'er-do-well fellows, and headed off to confront the strangers. His plan was to quickly subdue them and herd them off to the slavers who plied their trade on the south side of town. There he could get gold coin for the two, for they were rare breeds in these parts. A moment of indecision came to him suddenly as he remembered the unconcerned look of utter peace on the face of the messenger when he threatened him once before. It was as if the two had no fear at all, but he quickly dismissed it and hurried to catch them before some other did it before him. Then there were the bands of roving pleasure seekers to contend with who often preyed upon the weak and newly arrived in town. He himself had once been a part of that scene but had found that money brought both power and pleasure, so he had opted to pursue a life of gain instead. There were few, if any, honest men in Sodom. They all cheated one another, sought for the greatest advantage in any dealing, and would double cross anyone who stood in their way. Midsal hastened his step as he hurried to catch up with the pair first.

As he and his crew arrived at the market, his stomach dropped. A group of men had already confronted the pair and were demanding they disrobe. There was a quick burst of light and then they were simply not there anymore. Midsal had seen a similar trick from a passing magician once, so he knew that the two were close by – so he sent his men to search the market for the two. Hours later, when the pair had not been found, Midsal found himself feeling a begrudging bit of admiration for the two in their escape. But he determined that he would find them, so he reestablished his watch on the house of Lot. It was getting late, and a storm was brewing from the west, so Midsal left and returned to his lodging, a small room near the outer gates. He contemplated on the day's events and came to the conclusion that these men were worth more than a few gold coins, he could sell them in Gommorah for much more, for the slave trade flourished there. He felt like that all he had to do was get his hands on them first and all his future would be secure.

Abraham was worried. It had been almost three days since he had seen the Lord's messengers leave and head south. He had stayed in a constant attitude of prayer for Lot and his family. News had filtered back to him through the years of the wickedness of Sodom and Gommorah, a wickedness he had unwittingly contributed to when he rescued Lot and killed Chedorlaomer and his allies. Bera dominated the other cities of the plain now, and he was unscrupulous in his dealings and a known moral deviate in his personal life. He wished there was some way to get Lot out, for he did not have much confidence in his plea bargain with the Lord earlier. Abraham had sent men to warn his allies to steer clear of the whole area, for he suspected that God was going to make a clean sweep of things, and the whole area south of the Salt Sea was given to earthquakes and unusual sudden changes. He had done all he could, now all he could do was wait. He felt a strong breeze come in from the west as he stood on the bluff overlooking the south. He could taste the salt in the air from the Great Sea. He glanced that way and was alarmed to see massive storm clouds brewing and moving inland rapidly. The weather had changed in just a few minutes, and he knew that it was not good. He turned to go and made his way back to camp where he issued orders that all of the herds be bunched and kept tight through the coming night. He sent runners to the other camps and told them to double the stakes holding down their tents, he wanted none of his people exposed to whatever was coming their way. Now, all he could do was pray some more.

Chapter 18

Night came early, and with it, the two messengers who found Lot in the city gate and accompanied him back to the merchant ward of Sodom. They had no sooner arrived when a dark shadow across the way moved quickly away from the area and made its way to the room of Midsal near the outskirts of town. It was the same young boy who had informed him this afternoon of the messengers' departure from Lot's home. He pressed a small coin in the youth's hand and sent him to gather his cronies. A wicked grin spread across his face as he planned his next move.

Meanwhile, Lot, his visitors, and his family, along with his daughters' new husbands-to-be had just finished their evening meal. He told one of his daughters to bring water to wash feet when one the visitors spoke: "Do not concern yourself with such trivial matters this night, Lot, nephew of Abraham, favored one of the Most High God. We come with a matter of great urgency to discuss with you and your family.", said Eshael. "You are all in grave danger."

Lot replied, "What do you mean? Who is Abraham? My uncle's name is Abram."

"The Lord God of Heaven and Earth has changed his name to Abraham, for he shall be the father of many nations. His wife is no longer Sarai, but Sarah – for she shall bear him a son in due time.", recounted Eshael.

Lot sat down suddenly, it was too much to take in. Aunt Sarai was finally going to have a baby? It couldn't be, for Ziphah had told him years ago that Sarai's womb was dead. It couldn't be! And then he remembered the other words of the messenger. "What sort of danger are you talking about?", asked Lot.

Before he could answer, there came an insistent pounding on the door. Lot thought little of it. Traders and merchants were always seeking him out, for he had the best beef, wool, goat hair ropes, and goat's milk in the area. People were always wanting to buy what he had. He was tired, it had been a long day – and it was shaping up to be a long night, with the storm coming, and all. He hesitated, and then with a sigh, went to the door to see what these traders wanted this time. He opened the door and immediately knew that these were not traders seeking goods or services. There was an immense crowd of people around his house holding torches. The man Midsal spoke for the group, "Lot, we want the men who are in your house. Most of these people have never seen anyone like them, and we want to get to know them better." He said it with a chuckle and a wink, and Lot knew full well what this crowd meant by the inference.

"Men of Sodom, these men are under my protection, as given by the laws of hospitality. I cannot produce them for you. I have two virgin daughters, betrothed but not married yet, that I would rather give you than these men. Do as you will, but I cannot turn these men over to you!", said Lot.

"Who do you think you are? You come into our city and act like a judge over us. When we get through with your guests, we'll deal with you too! Now, we *will* take them! Come on , men, let's see what northern flesh feels like!", said Midsal, who had whipped up the crowd to cover his evil designs to first use the strangers, and then sell them.

Lot felt hands on his shoulders suddenly pulling him backward into the house. The door slammed shut and melted away into stone, as if it didn't exist. And none of the windows existed either. It was as if the whole house had suddenly become a block of stone with no entrances or exits. The crowd screamed in frustration as they searched high and low for a way to get into the home of Lot. It just wasn't there. Midsal was outraged. No, no, no! This could not be happening! It was another trick, like the magician's trick in the marketplace this afternoon. Little by little, people drifted away in disappointment, muttering about the turn of events. Most cast stern eyes at Midsal, as if it was his fault they got away. It was almost an hour later when Midsal realized that he was all alone in the street. Finally, he too, turned and went away.

"You are all in grave danger.", repeated Eshael. "Call your sons-in-laws and your daughters, get them out of this city, for we are sent by the Most High God to destroy the wickedness of this place. The sound of evil has risen to Heaven and God will utterly destroy the cities of the plain."

Lot's wife, Ziphah, listened intently shaking her head side to side. "Lot, I am tired of moving around. This is our home. These men can't be serious. God would not destroy our home, our way of life."

Lot turned on her sternly, "Listen to me, woman! There is a time to argue and a time to obey. This is the time to obey, Ziphah! Get your things together. If God says He is going to destroy this place and we should leave, then we had better leave!"

Ziphah stood shocked into silence. Lot had never spoken to her this way before. She could usually wheedle her way out of him no matter what, but this time she saw a determined look in his eye that made her back down. She turned, weeping, and hurried from the room.

He turned to his daughters. "Tell your husbands-to-be that we are leaving, and that they are welcome to come with us. Tell them that Sodom will not be here tomorrow when the sun rises, and if they want to live, they had better come with us."

His daughters returned to the room with the word that their men both thought that Lot was losing his mind. The daughters themselves were not sure of Lot's sanity either. Lot commanded both of them to gather their things for a quick journey. Out of respect, they complied.

The night closed in around them and Lot made his way to see how Ziphah was doing. She was sitting on her pallet, wiping her eyes and folding clothes. She had packed nothing. Lot sat down beside her. "Ziphah, we must hurry if we are to salvage anything of our life here. Please, please pack some clothes and food for the journey. I will gather what money I can. We will still have the herds. All is not lost."

Ziphah wailed and spoke sharply back, "All is not lost! We still have the herds! That's all you care about, your stinking herds of goats and sheep and cattle! I finally have a home I want and now you say we have to go! Lot, honestly, I don't know why I ever married you! I am tired of moving!"

Lot gave her a moment to regain her composure and took her face gently in his rough, shepherd hands, "Ziphah, you married me because you love me and I, you. And because I love you, I am making you move this one last time... because God is going to destroy this place. Do you understand? And if we are here, we will be destroyed too! God gave us this chance to escape. These messengers came here for one reason and one reason only, to help us! We must listen to them! Did you hear their names, Ziphah? Eshael and Dunael! They are here to bring God's judgment and God's fire on the wicked! And it will come by dawn's early light – so we must make haste and get ready, and go." Ziphah paled as Lot spoke to her and she seemed to finally understand. She dutifully went about packing her things and then went to the see about their daughters. Lot heaved a sigh of relief.

"Time is of the essence, Lot, friend of God. We cannot delay our departure any longer.", said Dunael to Lot.

"Just one more moment, please! I am hoping my daughters' men will change their minds. Please, just a few more moments."

Dunael shook his head from side to side and held out his hand. "Take my hand, Lot, and grasp that of your wife and daughters, as well. Now!" Lot did so, and suddenly they were no longer in Lot's home, but outside the gates of Sodom.

He turned to the messengers, "Where are we to go?"

"Head to the mountains quickly, there you will be safe. Don't look back, nor stay in the plains surrounding the city. Flee to the high ground as quickly as possible."

"What about Zoar, what used to be called Bela before the war? It's a small place, we cannot reach the mountains in time! Please, let us flee to Zoar, for my family's sake."

Eshael looked briefly to heaven and then spoke, "We will spare this place for your sake. God will allow it. Now go swiftly and do not look back, lest you also be consumed!"

The four people scrambled quickly toward the east to escape the coming wrath of God. As the sun was rising in their eyes, they heard a crack of thunder, and saw a single bolt of lightning streak across the sky from the east to the west. They were thrown off their feet by the cataclysmic boom that followed. As Lot looked on in horror from the rear of their band, Ziphah, who was leading the way, stopped and turned to look back one last time at her home in Sodom and… died. Rooted to that spot, she transformed suddenly into a solid block of salt, before the bewildered eyes of her daughters and husband. Lot sobbed as he gathered his daughters to himself and made his way sorrowfully into Zoar.

Abraham rose early that morning. All night long they had expected the storm, and it had not come. Only hot wind and crackles of static electricity filled the air as the clouds continued to roll in from the west. He hurried to the bluff overlooking the southern plains and was dumb struck by what he was about to see. He watched as a single bolt of lightning forked into four and struck the cities of the plains and they simply… ceased to exist. He saw it and then he heard it minutes later, as the loudest boom he had ever heard shook him to his core. Fire was everywhere. The smoke of the plains was as if God had lit a fire under the very ground itself. Abraham covered his eyes and fell to his knees in shock and awe of the power of God. The concussion of the blast finally reached him and blew hot air and ash his way. The very ground trembled under his feet as he saw the Jordan run backwards and find a new solitary path to the Salt Sea. The land where the cities had been seemed to sink out of view as the salt waters poured southward into the former valley of Siddim.   Abraham could only wonder if Lot and his family had survived.

Chapter 19

Dealings with Abimelech

"We must leave this place for a time.", said Abraham to Sarah. "I will leave the flocks with Eliezar and the other men and just you and I will travel southwest to see if we can make contact with some of the caravan traders who travel from Egypt to Harran."

"But husband, are you forgetting the promise of God? That I will bear you a son in a year?", asked Sarah. She had regained some of her youthful beauty in the past weeks since the messengers of God had come through. It was as if time were moving backward for her. She had regained her joyful spirit and Abraham marveled at the change. She no longer looked wistfully at the children of the herders, or even looked with disdain at Ishmael and Hagar.

"All the more reason to re-establish some semblance of trade. Since the destruction of the cities of the plain, no one is traveling the Jordan road anymore. They are all taking the coastal road and giving this area a wide berth. There simply is no one to trade with left in this part of the country, except for the Jebusites. We must find new markets for our sheep and goats and the cloth we produce. Besides, I have yet to hear anything of Lot... and maybe someone in Gerar will have heard some news."

Sarah nodded with understanding. Abraham had sent men into the plains to hunt for Lot and his family, but they had returned with no word of him. Rumors abounded that someone had escaped the destruction of Sodom, but it was as if the mountains themselves had swallowed them up. Abraham refused to give up hope, however, and continued to pursue every lead. In truth, Sarah perceived this trip was as much a hunt for Lot as it was a trip to establish trade.

"Just the two of us? I would like that, Abraham. In fact, I insist that Hagar stay here and keep up the camp. We should be gone no more than a few months at the most."

"We can travel faster this way. I can put you on one of the donkeys to spare you the burden of walking." We should need no more than one more beast to carry our supplies. This way, we can come and go with little attention.", said Abraham.

"What of brigands, husband? Should we not have a guard or two along to help discourage the highwaymen?", questioned Sarah.

"You may have a point, my sweet. Let me think on it. Meanwhile, ready your baggage, as I want to leave at early light tomorrow."

"So soon?", she gasped. "I can't possibly be ready until the day after tomorrow.... There's just too much to do, Abraham! I have to ready the cloth samples for trade, I have your and my clothes to pack, we must smoke some lamb strips for the journey, the list goes on and on...."

Abraham laughed. "All right, woman! The day after tomorrow it is.... That gives me time to make sacrifice to the Lord God of Heaven and Earth before we go and secure His blessing on our journey.... And think about taking guards, as well." He grabbed Sarah and lifted her up by the waist. "I am wanting you all to myself for a time, my dear. If we are to have a child, we have to be working at it, you know....."

Sarah shrieked for Abraham to put her down, but he refused, she beat him on the back, and he finally lowered her into an embrace, which she protestingly fought at first, but eventually returned. He found her lips and they kissed. Sarah coyly remarked, "I didn't say they had to share a tent with us, did I?"

"No, no you didn't...", said Abraham. "I am so glad to see you back to yourself, my love, I have missed this side of you."

"Years of frustration at being barren and that sordid episode in Egypt robbed me of my joy and peace of mind, husband. Only God could give it back to me. I thank Him for His promise."

"Selah!", exclaimed Abraham as he gave his wife a final twirl before setting her down and releasing her. He slapped her on her bottom and said, "Now get to work, woman! We have places to go!"

The air was filled with the sweetness of harvest time; a mingled aroma of barley, oats, wheat, and corn rode the winds that blew from the west, winds that were used to separate the grain from the chaff on the hills of Canaan. Almost in contrast to the cataclysmic events surrounding the cities of the plains, the hill country was experiencing one of their best harvests in years. The shortening of the days were leading to a mellowing of the climate. Hot days of summer were giving way to cooler, more refreshing days.

Abraham, Sarah, and two of his trained men with their wives made their way slowly south and east toward Gerar. The two men, Imani and his brother

Shamil, had been chosen by Abraham as much for their even disposition and quick reasoning as their skill in arms, which was substantial. The two had been born into Abraham's service and were loyal to him without question. He knew he had but to say the word and it would be done. As they stopped to camp for the night, he thought to himself that now would be a good time to tell the entire small band his plans.

"We are traveling into a new area where my influence is not known. People may have heard of Abram, but now I am Abraham – that is the name I will use, and people will not immediately know it. Sarah is my sister and I am her brother. You two are our guards, for we are merchants seeking new trade routes and contacts for commerce. All of this is true, just not the complete truth.", said Abraham, noticing the alarm in Sarah's eyes at his announcement.

"Husband, must we play this charade again? I fear it will not help us if and when they discover the truth. If you think this is best, I will do as you say. But I do not have to like it. ", murmured Sarah.

"Sarah, you are my greatest treasure and I would not risk you for the sheep of a thousand hills. Trust me when I say that this will work to our advantage. People will not trifle with a merchant family. I intend for you to handle negotiations with the women and I will handle them with the men. Together, we will turn our flocks, herds and cloth into goods and food for all our people. And we will inquire as to refugees from the plains, subtly, in the course of dealing – so as to not arouse any suspicion. I must find out if Lot made his way west to the coast, for I feel in my heart that he survived the destruction of the plains."

"As you wish, my husband……. But I cannot embrace this role wholeheartedly. And ask yourself this question, what should happen if I, indeed, do become with child? The changes in my body will reveal that we are more than just brother and sister."

Abraham thought for a moment, realizing the truth of what Sarah said. "We will risk it. My hope is that we are in the coastal area only a few months, at most. Surely the Lord God of Heaven and Earth will protect us."

Imani glanced at Shamil, who returned the look with understanding. "Lord Abraham", said Shamil, "Wouldn't it be prudent to have our wives pose as handmaidens to Lady Sarah? While we travel, we can each return to our own tents. But when we reach a stopping place for trade or information, have them pitch the small tents next to the cook tent and have Sarah convert it into her *mishkan* until we break camp for the next town."

Abraham smiled broadly. "Insightful, my friends, insightful indeed." He strode forward and clapped both of them on the shoulder. "This is exactly why I chose you two brothers as companions on this journey."

"One final word – keep your ears attentive to any mention of refugees from the plains. Work the subject subtly into the conversation, never ask directly about Lot. I suspect that even the coastal area knew of the wickedness of Sodom and Gomorrah and understand that they were cursed and destroyed for it. Superstitious zealots might want to exact judgment on any survivors they come across. Make sure that you identify that we are originally from Harran, but dwell in the hill country of Canaan, lest we, too, become an object of suspicion. The main thrust of our trip is to forge new trade agreements and foster trust for trade, not generate more enemies."

The small band all nodded in agreement as Abram then instructed them to clasp hands while they prayed. He lifted his face toward heaven and said, "Lord God Almighty, bless our plans. You are great, You are mighty, You alone are the One True God. Aid us in our endeavors. Protect us in the way. Reveal to us the fate of our kinsmen who dwelt in the plains of Jordan before You, in Your righteous anger, destroyed the cities for their wickedness. Blessed be Your Name, which you have withheld from men, God of my father- Terah, God of Noah, Enoch, and Adam. We give You Praise! Selah!"

Chapter 20

"Abraham! It has happened! May God be praised!", exclaimed Sarah.

"What?! Are you with child? How can this be, so soon?!" , shouted Abraham.

"No, silly man – I am not with child yet – but the way of women has returned to me! I, who thought my womb was dead, find myself experiencing the monthly sickness of a fertile woman! May God be praised!"

Abraham sat down suddenly – "Woman, you caused my heart to skip a beat! Right now, when we are finally approaching the city walls of Gerar, a pregnancy is the last thing we want." Seeing her downcast look, he quickly added, "Of course, as soon as we get on the road back toward the hill country – we will take advantage of this great news!" He stood and strode over to her and gave her a quick hug.

Sarah brightened. "I am thankful to the God of heaven and earth for His blessing…. Even the cramping, which I once despised, for it signaled another month of barrenenss, is welcome now. Now, husband, leave me – I must make preparation for this time of defilement. You must move your things to another tent for the duration."

Abraham laughed. "Of course, my princess, we must maintain our ruse, in any case. Tomorrow is the day we will meet Abimelech, king of Gerar. I have sent Shamil on ahead to make the arrangements. If all goes well, we will not be here more than a month."

Sarah smiled broadly. "Let's make it six weeks, and then I will be at the peak of fertility again. We can expect the promised child next spring."

"Sounds like you have thought this all out. It will be good to finally hold the heir of promise in my arms." Abraham gave Sarah one last loving look and strode to the tent opening and, ducking down, left Sarah to her thoughts.

"That I have, my beloved, that I have….", she murmured to herself softly.

Abraham tore his robe, dropped to his knees and prayed, "Father God, I cannot believe that this has happened again! What am I to do? Sarah is in Abimelech's palace and he plans to make her a part of his harem of wives! God, I will do anything you say, I will make any sacrifice you desire, I will build altars to You and Your greatness without ceasing! Only, rescue us from this situation. Give me wisdom, give me knowledge, give me a word…. What shall I do?"

Only silence greeted Abraham's plea. Abraham stayed before the crude altar he had hastily erected, prostrate in the dust, until darkness took away his hopes and dreams.   This is where Imani found him the next morning, sobbing uncontrollably…… for God had not spoken.

Sarah was nervous. She knew she was probably safe for only a few days, for she had told her attendants, who revealed to Abimelech that the time of women was upon her. This was enough to dissuade most men from acting upon their carnal nature. She hoped this was true for the king of Gerar, as well. After all, he had fourteen other women to choose from, if he were struck with the need for companionship. From the first moment Abimelech had seen Sarah, she knew he wanted her. She almost revealed her true relationship to Abraham, but did not simply because she had promised her husband she wouldn't. What plagued her so was the look of shock on Abraham's face at the announcement from Abimelech that Sarah would become his next bride. Then she was led away, casting one last look at a defeated Abraham. She could not be angry with him though and she almost felt sorry for Abimelech, as well, for she knew that he would never have his way with her. She would take steps to insure that it never happened.

First, she clung to the promise of God that Abraham would have an heir, and that she would bear him that son. Next, she prayed that God would take care of the situation without bloodshed. Even now, she thought that Abraham might be trying to figure out a way to rescue her. She wanted her freedom, but not at the expense of Shamil or Imani's life. With little support here, Abraham was at a disadvantage to mount a rescue – so she was trusting in a different sort of deliverance, one that only God could bring. Finally, Sarah sent a note written in Abraham's own private script to her husband that she was well and that there was no need for him to be alarmed for a few days. She finished her missive with a reminder of God's promise to them.   Sarah was thankful that she had learned the letters that Abraham had shaped to communicate with his people. She found that it was not difficult to secure a feather for a quill and she had brought with her some small pieces of papyrus. She made her own ink from the fireplace soot and the oils they used to fragrance her bath. She sent her note by way of one of the king's servants, who did not understand a bit of what he was doing, for the note was hidden among some of the goods being returned to Abraham.   Now all she could do was wait.

~~<Θ>~~

Days passed and Abraham was called to the palace again. An agitated Abimelech confronted Abraham with the truth. "You deceiver! You introduced Sarah as you sister when she is your wife!", he spat.

"Oh, mighty one, I did not lie….. she is the daughter of my father, but not of my mother. She is my half-sister. But you are correct, she is also my wife.", replied Abraham, "How came you by this knowledge?"

"Last night, I had a terrible dream. The Lord God appeared to me and said that I had committed a great sin by taking the wife of another man, a holy man. He said that Sarah was your wife! I defended myself by saying that I had not come near to her – and He replied that this was the only reason I was still alive – if I had taken your wife as my own, He would have destroyed me!" "How could you do such a thing? You should have been completely honest with me! How can you justify yourself?"

"It is a strategy I thought of many years ago when I first left my home in Harran, which has worked to my good many times. My wife is very beautiful, and I did not want to come into an area that did not know or fear God without an advantage of some kind. Sarah's beauty is my advantage. It distracts while I negotiate. If people think she is unattached, all the more they are distracted. She is a shrewd negotiator in her own right. She has been able to close many a deal, without me even saying a word. Also, men have killed others for women far less desirable than Sarah. I think, though, this is the last time I shall not tell the complete truth, especially concerning my wife. These past few days have been distressing, not knowing her status or how I was going to make this right."

"I should say so! Take your wife, and her servants that I have given her, and here is a thousand shekels of silver for her discomfort. Also, I am giving to you cattle and sheep for your wife's sake. I do this, not because you deserve it, but because I *do* fear God and must make amends for my near offense. Imagine if I had taken her as mine? My nation would be cut off from the earth and you, my friend, would have the bloodguilt of it all.

Now go! Leave Gerar in peace, and return to your hill country. Our business is at an end."

~~<Θ>~~

Shamil was tying the last of the wares for which he had traded onto a donkey when a man lightly touched him on the shoulder. He whirled quickly, not knowing if it was friend or foe, taking the man off-guard. He stumbled backward. "Forgive my brashness, sir….. I hear you are leaving Gerar and I wanted to see if I could be of help." "In fact," he lowered his voice, "I would like to leave with you, if I may. Gerar is not a healthy place for one who escaped the cataclysm of the plains."

Initially annoyed, Shamil narrowed his gaze to assess the man who stood before him. He was an ordinary looking man of marriageable age. His clothes were threadbare, as if he had traveled far with no extra provisions. His cheeks were sunk in from having lost weight recently, and his face was sallow, as if he were not well. His eyes were bright, however, and despite his weathered and poor condition, he appeared to be exactly what he professed to be – a refugee of the plains. In fact, he had an innocent look about him that fostered immediate trust. But Shamil was no fool – he had been deceived before by people with this same sort of look. The man's last statement, though, warranted an inquiry at the very least, for this was the first such person they had come across in their travels, and he knew that Lord Abraham was anxious for some news of his missing nephew, Lot.

"Shamil is my name, guard and servant of Lord Abraham of the hill country of Canaan. What do you mean by the statement that Gerar is not a healthy place for refugees from the plains?"

"I am called Fasah. I am the only survivor of the children of Hanokiah, a merchant of Bela, which is now called Zoar. We had the misfortune of being between cities camping when the great destruction occurred. Zoar survived the destruction. Had we but been home, my father would have survived and I would not be homeless and adrift without a heritage."

"I don't understand… as the surviving son, you should have inherited all that remained of his goods and home in Zoar. How is it that you are here, a castaway, and bereft of any livable means?"

Fasah dropped his head. "You are correct in your assumption that I *should* have inherited it all. But when I arrived home, some days later, I was quickly accused of being under the curse of God, as I was not one of the favored ones *in* Zoar when the fire fell from heaven. The elders seized my property and gave me a water gourd and banished me to wander in the smoking wilderness that was once a veritable paradise. They are all mad! They think now that they will flourish and become a great city, since all of the others in the plain were destroyed. They assume that they were spared because of God's favor and have made the claim that He will now make Zoar the greatest city in the world!" He shook his head from side to side as he spoke. "That was many months ago, and I have made my way here, only to find that religious fanaticism is not limited to people of Zoar. I have been hounded by those who think I should have died, as well. And some who have taken it upon themselves to see that God's vengeance is completed, even if they have to complete it."

Shamil listened intently and made a decision. "I cannot give you permission to join us, only Lord Abraham can do that. But... I will bring you to him so that you can plead your case before him, as well. He is a just man, a righteous man, a good man. He serves the Lord God of heaven and earth. He will hear you and make his decision. Do not fear, he will not slay you, as some would. As I said, he is a just man who fears God and knows more about the cause of destruction than anyone else alive, for God warned him beforehand of its coming."

Fasah followed Shamil back to the small encampment that was quickly being dismantled and packed. Abraham looked at him strangely when he arrived with a stranger in tow, for this was not the Hebrew way of doing things. He knew something was up, for Shamil had never done anything like this before.

"What have we here, Shamil? Who is our guest? I am afraid that this is a bad time for hospitality, as we are hastening to depart at once, as Abimelech ordered."

Fasah blanched at the use of the name of the king of Gerar. "Oh, Lord Abraham", he said, falling down before him, "Please forgive this one's rashness at coming at such an inopportune time. I fear for my life here and would accompany you as a servant, if you would but allow it."

Abraham looked at Shamil questioningly, who said, "Hear him out; his story has the ring of truth to it. He is a survivor of the destruction of the plains. If he comes with us, perhaps he can tell us more of his journey."

Abraham immediately understood the situation and Shamil's unorthodox move in bringing someone to camp as they were departing. Abraham lifted the man up and dusted him off, "What is your name, son?"

"I am called Fasah, only surviving son of Hanokiah, a merchant of Bela, which is now called Zoar. I was cast out as accursed by God when I returned home after the destruction. I have wandered these many months looking for some place to live. No one wants an outcast, especially one whom people think is cursed by God."

Abraham snorted. "If God had wanted you dead, then you would be dead. No, He must have some reason for sparing you. Come with us. We will talk more on the way back to the trees of Mamre in Hebron, where my people are encamped."

Stunned, the man looked sideways at Abraham, "Hebron is the home of Lord Abram, the rescuer of the five cities and defeater of the four kings of the north. Surely, you are not he?"

Abraham smiled a weak smile. "Guilty, I'm afraid. My name was changed last year by the Lord God of Heaven and Earth, just before He destroyed the cities of the plains. He also changed my wife's name, as well. We are now Abraham and Sarah, no longer Abram and Sarai."

Fasah hesitated a moment and then blurted out, "Then I have news for you, my lord….news of your kinsman, Lot."

Abraham trembled slightly at his words and said, "Tell me! Is Lot well? Did he survive? What of his family? Where is he?" The questions tumbled out of Abraham one after the other.

"He is alive. Last I saw of him, anyway. I stumbled upon his dwelling place quite by accident. He and his two daughters are living in a cave in the mountains outside of Zoar."

"What of his wife, Ziphah? Was she with him?", asked Abraham.

Fasah shook his head. "He did not speak of her, and I saw no one save he and his twin daughters."

Abraham, saddened by the news and the obvious conclusion of Fasah's words, dreaded the thought of telling Sarah the news that, most likely, Ziphah was dead. "As soon as we get back to Hebron, your first task will be to lead me to this cave where Lot was last seen."

"Yes, my Lord.", came the simple reply.

Chapter 21

Lot's Story

"As glad as I am so see you, my uncle, I wish you had not made this perilous journey to find me.", said Lot.

"Why did you not send word to me of your predicament, my brother? Or come to the trees of Mamre... surely you know you have a home with me always", chided Abraham.

The journey had been difficult. Finding a safe path from Hebron to Zoar had been accomplished only by trial and error, with many switchbacks and dead end paths which led to vast broken landscapes too difficult to cross. The land was still dotted with areas of unending heat, bellowing from the bowels of earth as if the very earth were on fire. Vast areas that had formerly been level areas of grass and fields had become virtually uninhabitable. There were dead areas, too, where no life existed – not even insects. On the edges of these places, people would become sick and vomit after only a short time and one would have to hasten away to escape before being completely overcome by something they could neither see, hear, taste, feel, or smell. Some had not been fast enough – and their rotting bodies littered the landscape, warning people away. The plains had become a veritable horror zone, and Abraham was determined that they would not travel the eastern side of the Salt Sea ever again. No, they would find a better route home along the western shore.

"My shame keeps me from returning to Hebron, Uncle Abram. I have made foolish choices and now I reap the rewards of my folly."

I am now called Abraham, dear Lot. God changed my name last year, just before…." He hesitated to say it for fear of opening old wounds.

"…..the great cataclysm of the plains.", Lot bitterly finished the statement for him. "Yes, I had forgotten, the visitors who rescued me told me of your new name. I suppose I owe my life to you, since you sent them to find me and keep me safe." He laughed hollowly, "They warned us not to look back, they told us to flee quickly and not look back…. But Ziphah couldn't let go. She had to see her home one last time…. And God killed her for it. Turned her into a pillar of salt…. right before my eyes." He pounded his hands into the crude table set before him until it splintered into pieces. He looked blankly at his bleeding hands and gestured for Abraham to go. "Leave this place! Leave me to my exile and punishment! My daughters and I will survive. I want none of your charity! I lost it all in Sodom and I will *not* be an object of pity for the herdsmen of the great Abraham.", he said bitterly.

"At least let me take the girls with me back to Hebron – we can find them husbands among my herdsmen, they can have a life free of this cursed land. I appeal to you, nephew, let me take them back to Sarah, who will love them as their mother did and will see to it that they have a future…" he trailed off as he saw his nephew slowly shake his head from side to side.

"It's not that simple anymore, uncle, I'm afraid they have already closed the door to a normal life…. And I, unwittingly, aided them in their folly. They are both… with child… And I…. am the father."

Horror befell the face of Abraham, the man of God. Repulsed by such shocking news, he seemed to age ten years in just a moment. "How can this be?", he hissed. "How could you have done such a thing? This is depravity and wickedness beyond my imagination."

Lot hung his head with shame. "In my grief over losing my beloved, I drank wine. My daughters took advantage of my drunken state to lay with me and each conceive a child. I truly do not remember a thing…. I only know of it at all because they told that they did it to "preserve my name" when I confronted them about being with child. He laughed dully. "What a legacy, what a name I have to preserve! – No, go and forget me, my beloved uncle, I will never see your face again. I am abandoned by God, my lineage is tainted beyond repair. My sons who are also my grandsons, for I am sure that God will punish me by them both bearing me boys, will bear the stigma of my failures forever. I will live out my life in shame and do the best I can for the tattered remains of my family."

All Abraham could do was turn and go.

Chapter 22

Isaac

The midwife slapped the man-child on the bottom sharply and was rewarded with a lusty cry. She quickly snipped the umbilical cord with a small pair of shears and twisted a piece of red linen cord around the stump and knotted it. She then wrapped the child in a square of plain white cotton cloth and turned and handed the child back to Sarah, who was reaching eagerly for her son.

As soon as the cry was heard outside the tent, Abraham fell to his knees and lifted his eyes toward heaven and cried out, "Blessed be the Lord of Heaven and Earth for His mercy toward His people! Gracious is He to grant this child to a man full of years. I praise you, Lord God, for you are rich in mercy and longsuffering with us, the objects of your grace. May this child be both a blessing and be blessed in all the earth, as I have been. Great God of all, we praise you and give thanks to you!" All around him, his herdsmen and their families had followed suit and knelt before the Lord. He rose to his feet and approached the tent gingerly.

"May I come in now?", he asked cautiously, for this was a woman's domain, and though he was lord of the camp, the midwife was the ruling Lady of the birthing tent, and not even he could usurp her authority. The flap was flung back so suddenly that it startled Abraham and he stumbled backwards and would have fallen had not Ishmael, who was now a strong youth, caught him. Abraham looked at his firstborn gratefully and rubbed his dark locks playfully as he turned back toward the now open tent. The midwife smiled and suppressed a laugh at the sight of Abraham's anxiety. "He's a fine healthy boy – and his mother is already feeding him. Go, Lord Abraham, and see your son. Both mother and child are healthy."

Abraham rushed past her and knelt at the pallet where his wife and newborn child lay. The difference between his two sons was dramatic, not only in age, but in countenance, as well. Whereas Ishmael was dark and swarthy like his mother Hagar; Isaac, as the child was to be called, was fair of color and almost hairless at birth. Both sons had taken on certain characteristics of their mothers, it seemed. Abraham wondered if the baby would look like him, but it was too soon to tell. He squeezed Sarah's hand and gave her a grateful look. "My Princess, you have done well this day."

She sighed and replied, "It's about time, don't you think?"

He laughed and said, "He's worth the wait, my beloved, worth the wait."

Outside the tent, Hagar pondered what this birth would mean to her and her son. She hoped that nothing would change, but in her heart of hearts, she feared otherwise. She called and held her son close to her and told him quietly in his ear, "Do all you can, dear son, to please your father. This day is a joyous one for all but us. Do you understand? You are his firstborn, he must not be allowed to forget that. Our situation is tenuous, at best. As long as we retain Lord Abraham's favor, we will be treated well and you will inherit much, but I am sure that Sarah will have other plans. Grow, be strong, and do all a good son should do, my Ishmael. And I will keep the peace as best I can, in the meantime."

Abraham stood before his people and announced the news. "We must relocate the camp for a time. The flocks have used up the land here and it must recover. We will travel south and west toward the Spice Route. We will encamp in the remaining plains west of the great Salt Sea, land that has been shunned by others because of the Great Cataclysm that occurred. My scouts tell me the land will hold us, though we must dig many wells to water the flocks. Make ready to strike camp, we will leave in three days." Abraham was being generous in the amount of time to strike camp simply because they had been in one place for so long. They had camped near Hebron for years now, and this would be the first move since Isaac had been born. Sarah was not happy about it, but she understood the need. Isaac was a toddler now, he would soon be weaned and she was not looking forward to a trek south and all of the unknowns of making a new camp. Abraham furrowed his brow, it had to be done, regardless of the circumstances.

The days had turned to weeks, and Abraham finally called a halt to the slow move to make a new camp. He looked around and was satisfied that they could make this shallow basin a new home camp from which to operate for a few seasons. There was water and grass, the necessities for living the nomadic life of a shepherd. The climate was temperate in these lowlands most of the year, so the cold which made his bones ache would not affect him as much. They were within a day's walk of the coastal trade route and within a half day's walk of the old spice route that had led to the cities of the plains, Zoar being the lone survivor had grown and the route was once again being used by merchants. Abimelech, king of Gerar, whom Abraham wanted to avoid, laid claim to areas west of him. He had instructed his herdsmen to travel mostly east to dig wells, but they could not avoid going west, for their herds were just too large. They had done so and found water quickly and plentifully, just a few dozen feet below the surface of the land. Everything was looking good.

The people had worked hard and deserved a celebration, so when Sarah informed him that Isaac had finally been weaned from her breast and was eating food, he took it upon himself to declare a holiday for the camp. They killed a calf that had been fattened up just for such a celebration and Abraham called upon his trusted old servant, Eliezer, to make music for them to dance, for he was skilled upon the pipe, and his sons were skilled upon the stringed instruments. It was a festive affair with Sarah proudly showing Isaac upon her lap – and gifts were brought and given to him, mostly toys skillfully carved by the hands of the shepherds, who were ever competing among themselves to see who could make the best carvings. After all, the long hours in the fields go by quicker if you have something to do with your hands, so wood carving had become something of a professional pastime. In fact, it was how Eliezer had become so proficient on the flute, it was a hand carved pipe he had done himself years earlier and he had so perfected it that he had given up carving and spent his time playing the flute instead. "Besides", he was wont to say, "music calms the sheep."

Finally, it was Ishmael's turn to give his gift to his younger half-brother. Ishmael had been learning all he could about his father's business. He had learned to read and write the Hebrew script his father used to communicate with his herdsmen. He had proven himself dependable with the flocks, and had even recently successfully defended a ewe lamb giving birth against a lone marauding wolf. He had been fortunate, for the wolves usually travelled in packs, less often in pairs, but rarely alone. He wore the skin of that wolf proudly, for he had killed it with a gift his mother had given him. Few of Abraham's people used or knew of this device that Hagar called a bow, preferring the sling for distance killing and the sword, spear, or dagger for up close. Abraham eyed his elder son with pride. "He's growing up nicely,", he thought to himself, "he is a tribute to his mother's people, the Egyptians – who have been using the bow for hundreds of years. Who knows? Perhaps my people can learn this new skill from Ishmael. I see the benefit of it."

Ishmael laid his gift before Isaac. It was a crude carving of…. a wild pig. Sarah reacted as if slapped. "Take that vile thing away, you wretched boy!" Isaac, puzzled, took his offering back into his hands. "I know it's not very good….. I do not carve as much or as well as the older men… but it is the best I have.", he said, his eyes brimming with tears.

"You mock my son with your rendering of an unclean beast, forbidden to us by God.", she said.

Ishmael replied, "I knew not that the wild boar I watched and carved a likeness of was considered unclean by God. No one ever told me."

"Well, now you know!", spat Sarah, "If your mother spent more time telling you the right things, then you wouldn't be doing the wrong things!"

Ishmael hardened at the attack on his mother. "Do not speak so of my mother, she has taught me much more than you ever have. You have ignored me completely most of my life."

Sarah lowered her voice and eyed him suspiciously, "I am the wife of Abraham and you dare talk to me so? Why I have a mind to...." Abraham, who had been watching helplessly at this sudden turn of events, came to himself and broke in, "Now, Sarah, the boy meant no harm... he was merely defending his mother, and attempting to give a gift to his brother..."

Sarah flashed her green eyes at her husband and clinched her fists, "Don't you dare shield him after what he just did!" Sarah turned and marched angrily toward her tent as Abraham miserably looked on. The scene had unfolded in the midst of celebration, and now, the music stopped; people looked at one another questioningly, and slowly began to gather themselves and return to their tents. The festival had turned sour and everyone knew it. Abraham was dazed at the unexpectedness of it all. He followed his wife to her tent.

"Now, Sarah, you have gone and spoiled the day... and shamed me in front of everyone.", said Abraham to his wife's back, which was shaking with silent sobs. She whirled on him in anger and bit her lip to stop the retort when she saw the compassion and sadness in his eyes.

"Abraham, I am sorry for that. I did not mean to make a spectacle out of what should have been a day of great joy. But.... you do not know what I know. You do not see what I see. This half-blood Egyptian and his shrew of a mother would take all you have and leave me and Isaac nothing, were something to happen to you. By tradition and tribal law, Ishmael is your heir. And I am to blame... for his birth was my idea! It eats at me day and night, that *our* son, the son of promise... will have nothing when we are gone! Hagar will see to that. You must send them away. You must secure Isaac's future. I beg you, send them away!", implored a weeping Sarah.

Abraham, stunned by the suddenness and the passion of this request, shook his head from side to side. "I cannot, my beloved, Ishmael is my son too! I .... I.... love him with a father's love. Surely you can understand that, can't you? I would sooner cut off my left arm as to cut off my son from me."

"Then I have no more to say to you tonight, husband. Leave me to my sorrow and my worry. Send Shamil's wife, Biri, to attend to me and Isaac. I have need of her." She turned her back on Abraham in dismissal.

Abraham started to reply, thought better of it, and lifted the door flap of the tent and left. He turned and walked away to find Biri, who was standing just a stone's throw away with her hands on the shoulder of young Isaac, who looked up questioningly at his father as he approached. Abraham knelt in the dirt and took his son's hands in his, "Your mother misunderstood the meaning of Ishmael's gift to you. She thought he was mocking our ways because his mother is not of our tribe, and sees no wrong in eating the flesh of the pig, which we will not do. She is better now, go to her and comfort her, my son." He turned to Biri, "She has also asked for you to come see her, as well. She did not tell me why. Thank you for looking after Isaac while Sarah was…. indisposed."

Biri flashed a quick smile at Lord Abraham and hurried off to Sarah's tent with the toddler, Isaac, following close behind. Abraham sighed. "If I live another 100 years, I will never understand women.", he thought to himself.

Chapter 23

Ishmael

"Mother, I still don't understand what I did wrong.", said Ishmael to Hagar, "I have always thought of the wild boar as a noble beast, eking out a living in the wild, answering to no one, able to defend himself against predator while preying on no other animals. I thought it would be a grand gesture to carve the likeness of one for little Isaac."

Hagar looked at her son with a mother's sympathy for a child who has been wronged. "It is just that Sarah is looking for any pretense to get rid of us, my son. You acted out of ignorance, my boy, and surely your father knows that. He will continue to defend you in this little misunderstanding. I am sure of it." She hoped in her heart that her words, which she longed to believe were true, would resonate with confidence in her son's ears. Ishmael was 17 now, a young man – bright, strong and full of vigor. Hagar lived for her son. He was her whole world. Sarah had long since dismissed her from her duties as her handmaiden, so she worked around the camp helping first here and there, always with an ear to hear what people were saying about her son. What she had been hearing lately did not set well with her. She lived a simple life, taking no man as husband – even though many had offered, due to her great beauty. She had friends in the camp. And they whispered to her that Ishmael's position as Abraham's heir was in jeopardy. Many wondered what Abraham would do, since he had finally conceived a child with his one and only wife, Sarah. Everyone knew the story about Ishmael's birth, just as they knew the story of Isaac's birth. A day of reckoning was coming, as surely as the sunrise. Hagar could feel it in her gut.

~~<Θ>~~

Abraham! Abraham! Fear not for the man-child Ishmael and his mother, your servant. Do as Sarah said unto thee…. Send Ishmael and Hagar away. Do not worry, I will look out for him and make a great nation of him.

Abraham woke in a sweat with the words ringing in his head. The crackling fire of earlier had died down to glowing embers, yet still gave off enough heat to keep his bones from aching on the damp ground where he lay. He did not often sleep under the stars anymore. He thought back over his life, his early years outside of Ur with Lot, his later years in Harran with his father, Terah, and his mother, Cherah. Oh, how he missed them and their advice in times like these! But he knew well how to recognize the voice of God, so he gathered his robes around him, picked up his staff, lit a torch from the fire, and made his way to the tent of Hagar to do what must be done. Dawn was approaching in just a few hours, and it was best if she left at first light. He owed her, at the very least, a few hours to ready herself for the trip ahead.

"I am setting you free, Hagar. You and our son may leave at first light. You are no longer my servant.", said Abraham simply.

Hagar sat up, eyes brimming with tears, "This is how it is to be? Used and then discarded when your precious Sarah is finally able to do in her old age what most women can do in their youth? I and my son are to be dismissed like so much dust on your sandal, shaken off to settle back into the earth?"

"No, Hagar, that is not it at all. I am merely following the commands of our God who told me to do this. I fought with Sarah and told her I would not do this thing. Although conceived not out of love for you or lust for your body… I love our son, Ishmael. This is the hardest thing I have ever done, including leaving

Lot in a cave to wallow in self-pity. I fought with Sarah, but I *refuse* to fight with God. You both must leave at first light. I will gather provisions for you. I suggest you head back to Egypt."

Hagar's shoulders slumped in defeat. She knew that Abraham would not, could not, change his mind in this decision. In her flight from the camp years earlier, she had encountered the angel of God and knew Him to be mighty, knew Him to be greater than the gods of Egypt, knew that she had no recourse but to go.... And hope for the best.

She decided not to go to Egypt. She had enemies there who would capitalize on her misfortune. Once highly favored by Pharoah, she would now be seen only as a cast-off with a half-breed child, who would be shunned and ostracized by the people of Egypt. No, her fortune lied to the south and east. Perhaps she could make her way to the coast. Abraham's many scouts had reported back that there were settlements there where water was in abundance. When one ventured into the desert, one must always think of water. At first light, she took her son, Ishmael, with no explanation at all, and said they had to leave. Ishmael, though puzzled, did not realize the finality of it and thought they were merely taking a trip. It was only later that he would learn the truth.

Hagar was lost. Her sense of direction had left her and she wandered in circles in the wilderness of Paran for days. Ishmael implored with her to return to camp until she finally broke down and told him that they could not return, for they had been sent away by Abraham under the command of El- *Shaddai*, God Almighty. Her fear of God kept Ishmael from returning to kill his father, but he swore an oath to never forget how they had been mistreated. Their situation grew desperate as the water ran out. Ishmael sat down under the shade of a eucalyptus bush to rest from the burning sun while Hagar, under the pretense of searching for water withdrew some distance away, sat down, and wept uncontrollably.

Her sobbing was heard by her son, who cried out in anger to God, "What have I done to you that I and my mother should die of thirst here in the wilderness? I am the son of Abraham, your follower and priest. Why are we cast out? Why am I despised by you?"

Hagar suddenly heard the voice of an angel of God speak to her. It was the same voice she had heard many years before when confronted by the angels at the well, when she fled from Sarah's presence.

"What's wrong, Hagar? Do not be afraid, for God has heard the voice of the boy from the place where he lies. Get up, then help the boy up, and nurture him, for I will make from him a great nation."

Hagar stood up and looked out in the direction of the voice and saw, not a stone's throw from where she had sat down to die, one of Abraham's famous wells, newly dug by his herdsmen for the time when his flocks would come this way. She lifted up her hands to the heavens and thanked God for His mercy. With a new determined look on her face, she strode toward the well, the empty waterskin held fast in her hand.

Chapter 24

Beer- Sheba

Abraham was personally involved in the curing the skins of several goats with salt for the extended tanning process that would begin once the skins had dried. He thought it important that his people knew that he was not above manual labor, but he preferred to choose where and when. Abraham personally hated the skinning process and the malodorous and lengthy soaking, liming, bating, and scraping that took place before the skins could be used for everything from hair ties for the woman to water skins for the men. The Hebrews, as they were now always called, did their own tanning for the camp most of the time, for the women were particular when it came to leather. The soft goatskin was prized most of all for its supple softness that made it study, yet flexible enough, for the making of coats, the upper parts of sandals, and the best wineskins. Abraham had instructed the butchers to keep aside the goat brains for the tanners, who would slice them, let them dry in the sun, and then grind them into powder to be used in a solution that caused the hard salted leather to soften. He much preferred this method to the more common use of urine that most town tanneries used. You could always tell where they were, for you could smell the tannery long before you reached it. Even without the use of urine and dung, as most tanneries used, Abraham's makeshift tannery could not escape the stigma of smelling...bad. So Abraham avoided the place as much as possible, and contented himself to contributing to the initial stages of the process.... many, many paces away from the bating and curing vats.

He was just finishing up salting the last hide when a runner came and delivered him a message from Sarah. He frowned as he read it, for her message was that he had an important visitor waiting at the main camp, only she did not say who it was. He noticed a slight shakiness to the letters that indicated that Sarah was either in a hurry when she wrote or was distressed as she wrote it. He poured water over his arms and hands to rid himself of the vestiges of his labor and wiped his hands on a small towel he had tucked in his waistband. He questioned the runner, "How long ago did Sarah write this?"

The runner, who was just getting his breath, replied hastily, "Not long ago, for I saw her write it myself and ran as fast as I could to you."

"Did you see who the visitors were?", he asked.

The runner, a young man who had only recently been assigned as a messenger, seemed reluctant to answer.

"Come now! Issaner, isn't it? Answer me truly, no harm will come of me knowing ahead of time who it is. I am surprised that Sarah did not include it in the message."

Issaner seemed relieved as he spoke, "Lord Abraham, I know not the names of your visitors... only that they are important. One looks like a king and the other a military man. They arrived riding on horses with a small complement of soldiers as escort. They hailed the camp as friends and called you and Sarah by name. I think I heard one of them, the military man, called 'Commander' by one of his men."

Abraham pursed his lips as he thought. He spoke, "Well, now! We will just have to go see for ourselves who these men are who know me and my wife by name. You have done well, Issaner. Now, I have another duty for you... Rest briefly and then hasten to Eliezer's camp and tell him what you have told me. I dare not trust this to writing this time. Tell him, Lord Abraham wants him to gather his armed men and circle the camp, do you have that? They must circle the main camp to insure our safety. I think this visit will not lead to anything more, but it is always prudent to be ready."

Issaner brightened at the compliment and then grew somber at the seriousness of the task ahead. He said, "Lord Abraham, I am ready now to deliver your message. Only... where is Eliezer's camp from here?"

Abraham laughed and clapped him on the back. "My soul, I forgot you are new to this! Eliezer's camp is several hills to the north of here." He pointed in the direction that Issaner would have to go – "Follow the wadi as much as possible, stay to the low ground and skirt the hills, it is longer that way, but you will not tire as quickly – for it will take you until the sun is directly overhead to get there. You should run into some of his guards and shepherds long before you get to the camp. Here, show this symbol on this leather patch to identify yourself to them and to Eliezer." Abraham took his personal leather patch out of his shoulder bag and gave it to Issaner. On the square patch that had been dyed a dark blue was Abraham's name skillfully wrought in the script he himself had devised. He had had it made some time back for just such a need.

Issaner looked at the patch with wonder. He purposely had not been taught the script, nor its meaning. For security's sake, the messengers were selected from the untrained so they could not be forced to read what they carried to others, if captured by enemies. But everyone of the tribe knew that this was the symbol of Lord Abraham. That he was to be entrusted with it made him both proud and nervous at the same time. He hurried to leave, but Abraham stopped him, saying, "You might want to fill your water skin from the well before you go. It's a dry walk from here to there." Issaner thanked him, did so, and hurried off in the direction that Abraham had indicated.

Abraham picked up his staff, slung his own water skin around his neck and told the servants to finish cleaning things up and take the salted skins to the drying racks. He turned and headed toward the main camp.

As Abraham came into the camp, he spied in the distance the supple form of Sarah entertaining the guests with food. Biri had taken charge of Isaac, for it seemed that since the weaning – Biri, who had no children of her own, had been selected by Sarah to be Issac's tutor and guardian. Abraham thought her a wise choice, for she was one Sarah trusted implicitly, since she had been one of the ones who accompanied them some years earlier to Gerar and posed as Sarah's handmaiden. Thinking back to that time gave Abraham a shudder as he thought of how God had been uncharacteristically silent in his time of need. Without Sarah or his God, Abraham had truly felt alone in those difficult days.

As he came closer, he realized the source of Sarah's discomfort. Their guest was none other than Abimelech, king of Gerar! Abraham uttered a quick prayer to God for wisdom as he approached.

Sarah wrinkled her nose in disgust as Abraham strode into the camp. "The stink of the tannery clings to you! Get into the tent and change clothes immediately while I fill our guests' cups one more time."

Abimelech laughed a hearty laugh and rose to greet Abraham, "If I ever had any doubt that she was your wife, it is completely gone! Only a wife would say that to her husband in front of guests!"

Abraham clasped forearms with Abimelech and replied, "Yes, it is true what you say – and I had better comply with her demands if I want to eat supper tonight! I will be right back." After doffing his sandals and washing his hands in the basin outside their tent, he ducked quickly into their tent and found a change of clothes and some sweet oil to dab on his hands and neck to hide the odors that clung to his hair and beard. "Oh, I cannot bathe more – there is no time.", he thought – so he dumped more of the oil on his hands and wiped them through his hair and beard, as well. It was a subtle fragrance; so hopefully, it would not appear that he was vain. He disrobed to his small clothes and shoved the smelly pile of clothing under the back of the tent, so Sarah would not complain about him smelling up the tent later. He put on a fresh shirt of linen and his best robe.

After all, he was greeting a king and a commander. It never hurts to pay respect when respect is due.

Abraham emerged from the tent looking, and smelling, like a new man. Even Sarah was impressed with the transformation in such a short time. "Now, how about some of those victuals for me, as well?", he quipped. He rubbed his hands together in anticipation, for he dearly loved his wife's cooking. She did not cook much these days, just as Abraham did not tend sheep anymore. They both were simply too busy with other things to do the tasks that they grew up in.

"Oh, no... this is for our guests. I did not make enough for everyone to eat!", said Sarah, as she regained her composure and mock anger with Abraham. She shook her spoon at him, "You should leave the manual labor to others! I have told you a hundred times, and see... now we have guests and you are hardly presentable! Serves you right!"

Abimelech and the commander were trying hard to hide their mirth at Abraham's dilemma. They were unsuccessful. Finally, Abimelech rescued a downcast Abraham by saying, "Here, Sarah, give him some of my portion. I cannot stand to see a grown man looking so glum. I will share your savory stew with your husband, although it is like giving up a rare treasure again." He winked at Abraham as Sarah colored at the obvious reference to their earlier meeting in Gerar.

Sarah, silenced, took a clay bowl and set it front of Abraham and ladled him a small portion of the stew, which was composed of goat meat, lentils, and spices from Egypt that Sarah carefully horded for special occasions. The stewpot looked like it held enough to feed a small army and gave off a wonderful smell. Abraham started to protest his small portion, but realized the futility of it when Sarah turned and instructed a servant to feed the rest of Abimelech's men from her stewpot, as well. She would triumph in this war of the sexes, as she usually did. He would get his revenge, however. He just had to bide his time.

"I have come to make a treaty with you and your people", said Abimelech. Abraham silently gave a sigh of relief. "Swear to me that before the Lord God of Heaven both here and now, that we will be friends and that you will not rise up against me or my people while you dwell in my lands."

Abraham thought on it and replied, "I thought your lands were to the west of here. I settled in what I supposed was open country, abandoned by the peoples of the plains after the cataclysm."

"I understand your thinking, Abraham, but you are mistaken. My father made claim to the land from Gerar to the Salt Sea, a claim I intend to enforce. I come in friendship, for I have come to believe in your God. Swear to me that you will not deny this claim and you may live in peace in the land."

Abraham thought briefly and came to a conclusion, "May it be as you have said. I swear to uphold the peace between our peoples. Only, I have recently heard reports that my men have been turned away from the wells which we have dug to the west. I can only assume that your men are the ones who have turned us away from our own wells."

Abimelech turned to his commander and said, "Phicol, is this true? Have you set guards upon the wells that they dug?"

Phicol replied to his king, "We knew not who dug the wells, only that they were dug without your knowledge, so until ownership could be established, we turned away all who attempted to use them."

"This is the first I have heard of this. I should have been notified sooner of these wells, Phicol.", rebuked Abimelech.

"Yes, Lord. I was remiss in my duties, it won't happen again.", said Phicol.

"You are to cease guarding these wells from the shepherds and tenders of Abraham. I know that he who controls the water controls the land, but Abraham is our friend, and we will trust him with this part of the land as long as he desires to live here.", announced Abimelech.

"Yes, my King.", came the swift reply.

Abraham sent word for Eliezer and his men to return to their flocks and also for a gift of cattle and sheep to be brought for Abimelech, as was customary in sealing treaties of alliance. He went one step further, however, and had seven ewe lambs separated from the rest and brought to his tent.

"What are these lambs for, Abraham?", questioned Abimelech.

"As a sign of our agreement, and of your recognition of the well we have dug here in this place, I ask you to take from my hands these seven ewe lambs.", he said solemnly to Abimelech. He picked the lambs up one by one and handed them to the king, who received them and sat them on the ground behind him.

Abimelech replied, "May our peoples never cease to be friends, my descendents and yours, forever."

Abraham smiled. "One can only hope, my friend, one can only hope."

"Come, let us return to Gerar, Phicol. We have other sheep to shear…literally.", laughed Abimelech.

Abraham, having one final thing to say, raised his hand and said, "This place shall be known as Beer-Sheba, the well of the seven, for we have made our pact here."

"I like it, my friend, Beer-Sheeba… of Philistia – for that is what we are calling this land from the coast to the Salt Sea.", said Abimelech, as he mounted up with a flourish. He reined his horse and turned to go, looking once more at Sarah with a sad nod, he then rode off to the west in a cloud of dust.

Some years later

Abraham shook the dirt off his hands as he finished planting the small tree next to the stone lined well in the camp. He turned to his son Isaac and said, "Now, we are making shade for the future. When people come to this place they will not only be refreshed by the clear, cold water from the well, they can rest in the shade of this tamarisk tree from their travels. The Han-Negeb is hot and dry, and travelers are thirsty and tired. We will make this place more than just a place to rest. People will come to this well and settle here, for the water is good, this tree will absorb the salt from the ground and bring it to the surface, where the cattle and livestock can lick it. Trees make a place come alive."

Isaac looked up at his father with shining eyes. He clung on every word his father spoke. He knew his father was a great man. Even as a young child, he could sense his father's importance. He wanted to be just like him.

Chapter 25

The Great Test of Faith

Abraham was getting stiff and sore. The years were catching up to him. Even Sarah was beginning to look more her age. It had been years since he had seen Lot, or Nahor, or even heard from them. Nahor had moved to Harran after the death of their father and stopped sending caravans south. He wondered if his kinsmen still lived. Every day was like the other, a routine of tending to business. God had continued to bless Abraham. Quite possibly, he had more cattle, sheep, goats, donkeys, camels, and true wealth than many of the kings of Caanan. He knew that the favor of God was upon him and his people. Occasionally, he would hear news of his eldest son, Ishamel, who had settled in Paran near the coast. He heard that Hagar had sent for him a wife from Egypt, he had not been invited to the wedding. He also heard that Hagar had finally married a spice merchant near the gulf and secured her future. He was glad for her. She deserved a measure of happiness, for she had been a good and loyal servant, despite her clashes with Sarah. He sent a wedding gift to his son of a herd of cattle and a flock of sheep, but they had been returned, the gift refused. He sent gifts of gold and goods to Hagar, which she accepted. He pondered sadly over what might have been.

Isaac was a youth now, growing into his manhood. His twelfth birthday was coming up very soon, and Abraham wondered what Sarah had planned for this commemoration of passage from childhood. He knew that she was grieving over him leaving the tents of the women to take his place in the world of men, but at the same time – she was proud and eager for her son to prove himself in that world.

Abraham had been careful to school him in the family business. He had started with letters and tallies. One must know how to count beyond their fingers and toes to raise herds of livestock, and Abraham had substituted his Hebrew letters for the straight marks that most tally men used to count. All of his business utilized the same method, for it only made sense to do so. But he still had to teach Isaac how to recognize the reckoning marks of the caravan merchants, and the Egyptians, and the Sumerians, and the Philistines, as well. There was so much to know and Abraham was going to make sure that Isaac's education was not lacking in any way. He was not going to fail Isaac, if he could help it. He felt, though it was no fault of his, that he had somehow failed Ishmael.

They had dwelt in Beer-Sheba for almost a decade, it was beginning to feel like home. His words to Isaac earlier when the tree was planted had proved to be prophetic, for travelers had come and built homes near the well of Beer-Sheeba, resulting in the makings of a real, although small, town. Abraham didn't mind, for this land was claimed by Abimelech, his friend. He thought back of how their friendship started and wondered at the mercy and goodness of a God who could turn a potential enemy into an ally and friend. All in all, He had led quite a blessed life.

"Abraham!"

The voice was so loud in his head that it woke him up. He rose from beside Sarah and made his way outside. This was not an unusual occurrence for him to go out to view the stars, so Sarah was used to his frequent nightly talks with God. He strode quickly to his favorite knoll and knelt and looked up to the sky and said, "I am here, Lord… speak, that I may obey."

"Abraham! Take your son, your only son Isaac, whom you love, and go to the land of Moriah. Take him and offer him as a burnt sacrifice unto me on one of the mountains there which I will show unto you."

Abraham, stunned, fell onto his face before God. Speechless, he lay there, tears streaming down his face at this awful command from His God. He dared not question God, he dared not disobey God, he dared not bargain with God, as he had done for the life of Lot. He was older now and saw the folly of trying to do anything except simply obey the Lord God of Heaven and Earth. His mind went blank and he fell into a deep dreamless sleep that only abated at the first gleam of sunlight the next morning. He woodenly rose from the ground and made his way back to his and Sarah's tent.

As he pushed his way into the tent, Sarah turned and saw him enter. She immediately knew that something was troubling Abraham deeply. She also saw that he was not ready to talk about it. She rose gracefully from their bed and embraced him, despite the dust which clung to his robe. She looked into his eyes, eyes clouded with impending worry, and spoke, "My husband, I can tell you are troubled. I can tell that God has spoken to you in a strong way this past night. And I can also tell you need to think on what He has said without any complications from a nagging wife."

Abraham gave her a weak smile.

"But… know this, my husband; I am here and ready to hear what God has said whenever you are ready to tell me.", she finished.

Abraham hugged her fiercely, his eyes misting with tears. "What did I do to deserve such a woman?", he exclaimed. "Sarah, I *will* tell you what God has said…. At least part of it. I am saddened that it comes so closely to our son's birthday. We will have to forgo the celebration, for now. I must leave…. and… I must take Isaac with me… and travel three days journey to the north…. there on the mountains of Moriah, Isaac and I are to offer sacrifice unto God."

Sarah sat back down. She could see that there was more than he was telling. You do not live with a person for over seventy years without getting to know that person well. A fear struck her heart, but she refused to believe in it. She smiled back at her husband, "Well, that's what you will have to do then. We will just have to celebrate when you both return in six days."

"I must leave today….. as soon as we can make ready. I will take Shamil and Imani with me, for protection. We must take the firewood and the sacrificial preparations with us. I will load up a donkey with split wood. I must do the work myself. Please make sure we have provisions for four for a week. Dried meats and shepherd's bread, the flat unleavened bread that keeps so well, will do. We will hasten there and back as quickly as we possibly can."

'I will be waiting, my beloved husband, I will be making final arrangements for our son's celebration.", she said.

Like a dagger to his heart, her words pierced him and he struggled to keep his composure. He could not tell her the whole truth. He would spare her those details until he returned…alone.

"Father, it is such a long way… cannot I ride upon the donkey?", queried young Isaac.

"If these old legs can make the trip, my son, then your young ones will do just fine.", said the doting father; who in truth, would have usually allowed it, but wanted the trip to Moriah to last as long as possible. He was in no rush, for he prayed every minute that God would change His mind and relent from the deadly command.

Isaac, disappointed, said, "Well, what shall we talk of on the way? I am tired of tallies and letters, teach me something new, father."

Abraham brightened, "That is what this whole trip is about, son. God is teaching both of us something new. Did I ever tell you of my only trip near to where we are going?"

"No, father, you have not. I have heard of Hebron and Shechem, but not of Moriah."

"It is nearly halfway between the two – there is a city near there, ruled by a mysterious king named Melchizedek. I met him once. He, too, is a priest and follower of the One True God. No one knows his lineage, however."

Isaac stopped walking. "But…. surely someone knows…. He had to have a mama… didn't he?"

Abraham laughed. "I forgot how literally children take things….. of course he had a momma, everyone has, or had, a momma… except father Adam, the first man… who was created by God Himself out of the dust of the earth."

"I remember that story. Mother told it to me. It is one of my favorites. And also Eve did not have a mother either…. She was created from part of Adam."

"Correct, my son…. I am glad you have been paying attention during your lessons on our history. Can you be more precise? What part of Adam did God use to make Eve?"

"A rib…from Adam's side!", the young boy said excitedly.

"Also correct. Well said, my son.", said Abraham, who hid his dark thoughts behind a cheerful countenance. He so enjoyed this, traveling once again, seeing old sights. They would have to stop and camp by the trees of Mamre near Hebron and there tell young Isaac of the destruction of Sodom and Gommorah. He furrowed his brow suddenly, he would not tell him about his cousin Lot's involvement in the great cataclysm…. that could wait until he was a little older. Then it struck him… if everything went without a change, Isaac would never *be* any older. He sagged his shoulders suddenly at the thought, but straightened up quickly. No need to alarm him, nor Shamil and Imani. He must make as if everything is going well.

There were few travelers on the road this time of year. It was the late spring and most were busy planting crops or grazing their herds… fattening them up on the lush grass that grew so quickly after the early rains. There was the occasional caravan of traders – they traveled year round – but for the most part, they had the road to themselves as they made their way northward toward the hill country. Isaac had a thousand questions, and when Abraham tired of answering them, he sent him to Shamil, who later sent him to Imani. It was Isaac's first trip of any sort from the south, and he wanted to make the most of it.

When they finally made camp for the night, Abraham lay back on his pallet and looked at the stars and remembered God's covenant. *"Your descendents shall be as numerous as the stars of the sky."* Abraham could only hope it was still so.

That night he dreamed of his younger days in Ur. He remembered the horror his father Terah had expressed at the prospect of human sacrifice. He saw, as an observer, the promise his father exacted from him… the passion of Terah burned indelibly into his mind, "….on my travels, I would come across high places dedicated to Molech still smoldering with the remains of children on the altar! Precious children! I can think of nothing that upsets me more than to think of God's greatest gift to us, allowing us to participate in His creation of life by having children, being abused and burned upon a pagan altar to a fictitious god! Promise me you will never do such a thing! Promise me!"

And then he saw himself, younger, self-assured, saying, "I promise, father – I can think of no greater sin than to kill one's own beloved child. I cannot fathom it!"

He woke in a sweat, trembling at the vivid memory of what had happened over eighty years prior…… He rolled over onto his knees and whispered quietly in prayer, "Dear God, I must choose now between obedience and disobedience of the will of two fathers…. You, who are the Father of us all, who have asked me to sacrifice my son, and my promise to my earthly father, Terah. I swore I would never do what you have asked. It never occurred to me that you would ask me to do this. If this is a test; please, Lord God, let me out of it. I am in agony, my Lord. I am undone. Take me, and let my son live, I pray. Only this once will I ask and if you do not answer… know this, I will obey your command."

All the answer he received was the chirping crickets of the night.

The next morning, as they reached the trees of Mamre, Abraham was saddened by the news that his old friend, Mamre, who had fought alongside him against the four kings of the North, had died just a few days prior. In fact, his widow thought he had come to express his regards and insisted they stay the rest of the day to mourn with her and her family. Abraham was in a quandary, knowing that God expected him to finish what he had started as soon as possible. He had also told Sarah that it was three days journey to Moriah. She would be expecting him home within a week. They could still make it, but it would be tight. He told Mamre's family that he had vowed a vow to the Lord God to make sacrifice in Moriah. He then promised to stay an extra day on the return trip to mourn Mamre properly. They understood, and let him go.

The trip hastened now, Abraham relented and allowed Isaac to ride the donkey in front of the stack of split wood that Abraham had prepared before leaving Beer-Sheeba. On top of the stack, wrapped carefully in a scarlet linen cloth, was Abraham's sacrificial knife. The same flint blade he had used countless times before to kill lambs, goats, and bullocks. This knife was old, older than Abraham. His father Terah had used it in Ur and later in Harran. It had been a parting gift from father to son, when Abraham left to follow his God's command. The cloth the knife rested in had been one of the last pieces to come from the loom of Cherah, his mother before her death. His father had given it to Sarah, but Abraham had asked her for it, knowing that she did not like the color…. besides, it made the perfect wrapping cloth for the knife. The two complimented each other, symbolizing the love and struggles of his own parents, and their final gifts to their son. Abraham had planned to give the knife to Isaac, when the time came….. only not in the way that God now demanded.

The second night found them just a short half day's journey from Salem, the city of Melchizedek. The two brothers were happy at the prospect of the journey's end, for they had not let their guard down once during the trip, and the stress was beginning to show on them. They sensed that there was an urgency to this trip, but could not quite put their finger on what was troubling Abraham. The normally taciturn Imani even spoke up once and quipped, "I'll be glad when we get there tomorrow. This trip has been different from what I had imagined it would be."

Isaac raised his head from his chest and nodded, "Me too! I am ready to go home."

Abraham, silent, fed the fire and did not comment. His hollow eyes told them all that he was ready for it to be over too. Only Shamil seemed not to notice the mood, "Well, perhaps we can stop by Salem for some wine to take back to the celebration of Isaac's birth – the grapes of the hill country far outstrip the sorry excuse for the ones in the south. I can't wait to get a taste, for it's been years since I had any good wine!"

Imani nodded in agreement and the conversation tapered off. Abraham finally spoke, "Get your rest, tomorrow we arrive at the mountain of sacrifice."

"Stay here with the donkey, the boy and I will continue the rest of the way on foot, alone.", said Abraham to his two men. "The boy and I will return when we are finished."

They nodded, not understanding, but used to obeying Abraham, even when they did not know his mind. They watched as father and son struggled under the load of split wood, wondering why it had to be hauled all the way from Beer-Sheba to Moriah; and now, why it had to be hauled another few miles to the mountain by sheer man power alone. What was going on? Abraham, normally a festive spirit, had become increasingly somber as the trip had gone on. Perhaps it was the death of his old friend, Mamre, that had cast a pallor over his personality. They looked at one another questioningly, and both realized at the same time that something was missing.

Shamil spoke first, "Did you notice something strange, brother?"

Imil answered, "Yes, yes I did…. I just realized that Abraham brought wood, his knife, and even took a faggot from the fire for the burning of the sacrifice… but…. where is the sacrificial lamb?"

"I don't know, brother, I don't know."

~~<Θ>~~

The same question was burning in the mind of Isaac as they approached the foothills. Near the end of a mountain was an outcropping of rock, vastly different from its surroundings. It was near to the walls of Salem, but separate from it by several hills and wadis. It appeared to be a place where, in the harvest, the people would winnow grain – throwing it up for the wind to separate the wheat from the chaff. It was abandoned in the spring, and it seemed to be their destination.

Isaac quietly spoke, "Father?"

"I am here, my son.", answered Abraham.

He questioned his father, "I see we have the wood, we have the fire, but we did not bring anything for the burnt offering. Father, why did we not bring a lamb to sacrifice?"

Abraham's eyes misted again, "God Himself will provide the lamb of sacrifice, my son."

When they arrived, Abraham sent Isaac to fetch the stones they would need to build an altar. Abraham constructed the altar numbly, without thinking, without emotion, just as he had done so many times before, and laid the split wood upon the altar. He motioned his son to come to him.

"I must obey God, my son. Do you understand this?", said Abraham to the trembling boy, who was just beginning to understand the situation.

"Yes… I do… father…", he choked back. The realization then came suddenly to him that *he* was the provision God had made, *he* was the child that God had given to a childless couple, *he* was to be a sacrifice. He thought about running away… he did not want to die. He had seen his father slay the lamb upon the altar many times, and he did not want to *be* under his father's flint knife. His father was old, he could not catch him. He could run away and hide and make his way back to his mother who would protect him. But… he looked into his father's eyes and saw the agony there… and knew that he could not run. He loved his father too much. And he hoped against hope that his father would love him more than obeying God. He decided to stay and to die if need be… for his father's love.

Abraham took the hemp robe from his waist and bound Isaac firmly with it. With a strength that belied the old man's frame, he lifted his son up onto the waist high altar and laid him there. He unwrapped the ancient knife that had spilt the blood of countless sacrifices and laid the red cloth aside. The burning torch was shoved into a crack in the rock floor by his side. As Abraham was doing these things, a cloud covered the sun and the landscape darkened. Although it was barely noon, it seemed as if it were the time of evening sacrifice. Abraham lifted the knife high above his head and looked into the eyes of his son, his only son – God had called him, indicating that this was the son of promise, this was the heir, the one who would follow God. Abraham almost began to falter when he thought, "God has never lied to me – if this, my son, should die by my hand this day…. God will raise him up. He will make him alive again!" Strengthened by this realization, He began the downward thrust, when suddenly God, through one of his angels, spoke:

"Abraham! Abraham!"

Abraham replied, "I am here."

"Do not lay a hand on the boy or do anything to him. For now I know that you fear God, since you have not withheld your only son from Me."

Abraham looked up and saw a ram, caught by his horns, in a thicket. Joyfully, he took his son down from the altar and loosed his bonds and told him to run and tie the rope around the ram's neck and wait for him.

He stunned the ram with his staff, knocked him down and tied his legs with the remainder of the rope and the two of them carried the ram to the altar where Isaac, just moments before, had lain.

He lifted the knife once again and said, "The Lord Provides!" in a loud voice – and plunged the knife into the throat of the ram quickly, efficiently, as Isaac took the burning torch and shoved it under the wood. Abraham then took the scented oil and threw it onto the small flame, where it blazed into life, consuming the ram and filling the air with the familiar smell of a sin offering.

Abraham turned and embraced his son, "Did I not tell you He would provide? Did I not tell you He is a good God? Did I not tell you that if we but trust Him, He would answer in mighty power?" With tear streaked cheeks, Abraham turned to face Salem, the city of the mysterious king and priest Melchisezek, and shouted at the top of his lungs, "Praise Be to the Lord God of Heaven and Earth! Praise Be to the One Who Provides! Praise Be to God! Praise Be to the One True God!" The sound of his voice echoed back upon them as the angel of Almighty God spoke once again:

"This is what the Lord declares, 'By Myself I have sworn, because you have done this thing and have not withheld your only son, I will indeed bless you and make your descendents as numerous as the stars of the sky and the sand on the seashore. Your seed will possess the gates of their enemies. And all the nations of the earth will be blessed by your children because you have obeyed My command.'"

Abraham laughed and clapped his son on the back. He then lifted him high to ride on his shoulders, as he turned to go back the way he had come, toward home and… Sarah.

~~The End~~

Steve Loggins is the Associational Missionary of the North Jefferson Baptist Association in Mount Olive, Alabama. He is the husband of Kellye Waits Loggins, father of three children, Rebekah Loggins Parr, Laura Beth Loggins, and Micah Loggins and the proud grandfather of five grandchildren; Olivia Raye Parr, Levi Joseph Parr, Benjamin Charles Loggins, Elizabeth June Loggins, and Hattie Ruth Loggins. This is his first literary work of fiction, but his extensive poetry blog can be found at http://poemsoneternity.blogspot.com.

Made in the USA
Coppell, TX
02 January 2020

13962752R00075